Praise

"If *Hellraiser* and Netflix's *Castlevania* hooked up and had a trio of queer poly bad-ass lady babies . . . well, hanging out with them probably still wouldn't be half as fun and scary and exciting as the wild ride that is *Glorious Fiends*."

— Sam J. Miller, author of *The Blade Between* and *Boys, Beasts, & Men*

"An unapologetically blood-soaked and darkly humorous read."

— A. C. Wise, author of *The Ghost Sequences*

"*Glorious Fiends* is about accepting your friends for who they are, even if they be liars, murderers, and inconveniently horny . . . Stufflebeam engages us from the start with monsters at their gory best (or worst, depends), pairing unexpected humor with shocking imagery that will turn your giggle into a shriek."

— Chris Panatier, author of *Stringers* and *The Phlebotomist*

Glorious Fiends

BONNIE JO STUFFLEBEAM

Underland Press

This book is published by **Underland Press**, which is part of Firebird Creative, LLC (Clackamas, OR).

Newly minted monsters are the worst . . .

Edited by Darin Bradley
Book Design and Layout by Firebird Creative
Cover art by Chris Panatier

This Underland Press trade edition has an ISBN of 978-1-63023-066-1.

Underland Press
www.underlandpress.com

Glorious Fiends

For *William*, my favorite fiend

Chapter One

As far as Roxanne could gather from the books she scoured within the stacks of the Great Library of Evil, there were five ways to resurrect a murdered monster. Roxanne paced the dusty library floor. Each method held a sense of the dramatic. As she sunk her teeth into the fresh heart of her latest victim—the woman who had listened for an hour to Roxanne's tale of grief had housed such a tender heart—Roxanne ruminated over the choices for the hundredth time.

Her first option: she could stitch her friends, Mx. Hyde and Medusa, new bodies out of old parts. She could spread them on an operating table and wait for lightning to strike. Roxanne would look amazing bathed in a lightning flash, and how she would command her squad of ghoulish creepers! But Mx. Hyde would never let Roxanne hear the end of it, trapped in such a hideous form, and Medusa, well. Roxanne kicked the stone head left behind after Professor Abraham Lee Vansing's victory over the Monsters Three. Plus, it was Mx. Hyde who did the mad scientist schtick.

Roxanne sighed. There was always a ritual summoning of some demon to take care of the resurrection. She glanced over the books crammed two stacks deep into the spiderweb-covered shelves that stretched all the way to the ceiling. A librarian was rumored to live in the library and care for the books, but Roxanne had camped out in one room of hundreds within the enchanted archive hidden deep in the mystical woods and had seen no such librarian yet. If she had to read through all of the books herself to find the right spell to summon a demon, she might just join her friends in the afterlife.

She had tried using the power of love, but no matter how many times she knelt over Mx. Hyde's rotting body, she could not bring herself to cry.

Sewing the bodies into the trunk of a tree would be tireless work and required the assistance of a witch, but none of the witches who lived in the town appreciated Roxanne's lust for blood. The missing bodies were too often attributed to witches' work, which led to their burning, which led to the unfortunate waste of a good body to charred ash. Roxanne licked the last bit of blood from the heart in her hands and tossed it into the corner where she kept remains.

It would have to be the drop-of-blood thing. Roxanne leaned over the table where she had been whiling away waiting for the new moon. She touched the dried blood at the tip of the blade that had killed Hyde. She glanced at Medusa's severed stone head, her snakes frozen in their final act of hunger. These were the personal items she would need to soil with some human's blood. Soft piano cooed from the ever-present background noise. Roxanne didn't want to wait any longer. She'd already spent two lonely weeks in this dreadful place, the room in which her friends had died. For some stupid reason, it was the only place she could perform a drop-of-blood resurrection. Who made these rules? Probably the books could tell her, if she cared to look. The new moon was still one week away. She understood little about what monsters were made of, but she knew this: the first hour of a new moon and a drop of blood from a human would rescue monsters from their deaths.

"I hope you both appreciate me when you're alive again," Roxanne said. "I hope there's no more goddamned complaining when I request a fancy dinner every once and awhile." She shivered to recall the types of women Mx. Hyde preferred: the grungier and more easily forgotten the better. And forget Medusa; she preferred men. "You're both going to owe me big."

The journey into Lumberton was a long trek through underground tunnels broken open with tree roots and flooded with dirty water. Mosquitos buzzed around Roxanne but did not bite; they knew better than to feed on a fellow bloodsucker. Still, she waved her hands in front of her face to disperse their buzzing cloud. She hated the sight of little black dots in her vision.

She emerged from the tunnel near the river that snaked through the town center. She had memorized the path to the tavern by now. She was bored with it, bored with the whole enterprise of staying in one place. The town witches were furious about her extended stay. Roxanne passed one of their charred bodies and waved, then caught herself. "You're too lonely," she muttered under her breath. Despite the recent uptick in town murders, the foolish townsfolk had not eschewed the tavern or slowed their inebriation. They were bored, and hell forbid they give up booze in favor of safety. Roxanne felt a vague kinship with their frowning faces as she swept into the place. She was bored too.

She waited at the bar, side-eyeing patrons as she performed humanity. A woman with silky curls bounced from table to table. Roxanne bit her lip; the barmaid wore her corset laced so tight that Roxanne understood her to be a connoisseur of pain. She flirted with abandon. She would make a pretty victim, but Roxanne was saving her for a special occasion: her last town hurrah. Two skinny professor types shared a meal by an open window. A stout giant of a man enjoyed a mug of ale that was as large as his engorged liver must be. There were no other women in the tavern.

"What can I get you?" the barman asked.

"Is your wife here by chance?" Roxanne said.

The barman scowled. "Don't have a wife."

"Sister? Daughter? Mother?"

"What you getting at?" the man asked. "Don't have none of those either."

Roxanne sighed, scanned the room, and made up her mind. "I'll take your darkest beer."

The barman placed a ladylike pint glass in front of her. She slid him two coins and took her seat across from the stout man. She did not intend to walk the dirty tunnels again until she could do so with her friends, and the giant man looked like he ate enough meat to satisfy Roxanne's thirst for iron.

"Mind if I join you? There's nowhere else to sit," she soothed.

The man glanced about. "What do you mean? The place is empty."

"Nowhere to sit at all." She fake-sipped her beer. "What brings a man like you—" She frowned. "Seen any good skirmishes lately?" She shook her head. It had been a while since she'd fed off a man. She preferred to avoid them at all costs. "Beer, am I right?"

"I like a woman who drinks beer!" the man said.

Roxanne nodded and spoke as though to a child. "Yes, I like a beer."

"That porter you're drinking is a bold choice."

"I'm a bold woman," Roxanne said.

"Why are you talking to me like that?"

"Like what?"

"Like I'm a small lad," he said. "I brewed that beer, you know. I operate the brewery down the road."

"Fascinating!" Roxanne took another fake-sip.

"It's not for everyone," he said. "The porter. Want me to grab you something less intense?"

"Do you want to come with me?" Roxanne said.

"Where?"

"A bed somewhere," Roxanne said.

"Oh, I don't hire women of the night."

"This one's on the house, pal." Roxanne stood and grabbed at the man's hand. "I love a good brewer."

Roxanne led the man with his sweaty palms through the town's streets. He talked of brewing — fermentation and krausen and wort and yeast. Roxanne asked questions when he started to get suspicious, like when they entered the tunnel that led to the Great Library of Evil.

"Wait, are we going to wade through sewage? Just where do you live, lady?"

"Where do you get your . . ." She waved her hand through the air. He scowled. "The bitter stuff!"

"Hops? Oh, right then, I know a guy grows the finest hops you'll ever taste." He followed her inside the tunnels. "They're so flavorful. I like to make a tea with them too. Helps me sleep."

Once they arrived at the Great Library of Evil's giant black gate, the man marveled at the architecture.

"You must be from money," he said. "I'm sorry I suggested you were a lady of the night!"

"Come inside," Roxanne said and pulled him through the gate, through the garden, then through the door.

"It's late," the man said once they were inside. "Do you have trouble sleeping too?"

"I'm awake all night," Roxanne said. She bared her fangs and hissed. She clamped her hand across his screaming mouth. She pushed him toward the ground. He cowered. She pushed his head to the side and had her taste: like beer and the sweat of men. Roxanne tried not to gag as she took only as much as she needed for the night. She dropped the man, and he fell, eyes half-closed. She left him in the entryway to the Great Library of Evil.

Roxanne had come to this place with her friends. It seemed a lifetime ago. They fought the greatest monster hunter ever to walk the world. They lost.

Now Roxanne glided down the hall into the room in which they had fought their last battle, Roxanne and Mx. Hyde and Medusa. Her friends were the only two creatures Roxanne had ever trusted. The Great Library of Evil had not changed since the fight; the same massive spiderwebs were strewn across the corners, the same dusty books stunk up the stacks, and the same blood stayed soaked into the wooden floors. Roxanne ran a finger along the spine of *Mummy Murders*. Maybe one day the Monsters Three would leave behind their own diaries. First, they'd need to write them, then bind them, then curse them. Probably, Roxanne thought, most of these diaries were cursed. Roxanne shuddered, then yawned. Writing a diary sounded like a lot of work.

Roxanne wondered if her friends would remember death. For one week she wondered, in the pensive moments that snuck up on her, if her friends would remember her.

For one week, Roxanne paced. For one week, she drew portraits of curvaceous women in the library dust. She longed for the barmaid. She masturbated to thoughts of the barmaid. She took sips of the man in the foyer. She considered, then reconsidered, opening the books. Mx. Hyde and Medusa would likely chastise her for not taking advantage of the time to read, but Roxanne had never been a reader, not even when she was alive, and all the books were penned by monster men. For one week, Roxanne danced with a human skeleton she found in one of the adjacent book rooms. She pretended it was the bar-maid. She collected every spare tooth she found on the floor and built a little mouth. She made it speak. She inspected the strange footsteps that sometimes appeared in the dust. She binged one night on the man's blood and slept through the next night, overfull and bloated. She tried to tame a mosquito from the tunnels. She trimmed a hedge outside the library into a vagina. She pulled the petals off the flowers of the purple sleeping belle bean vines. She watched the seasons change in the span of a week, as they did near the Great Library of Evil. She laughed until she fell air-drunk into fallen leaves.

The night of the new moon, Roxanne rose with a spring in her step. She sat at the table that held the severed stone head of Medusa and the blade that had taken Mx. Hyde's life.

"It's time!" she told them, and she was convinced that they could hear her from the underworld in which they toiled.

She threw open the doors to the evening, stood in the entryway, and blew a kiss to the darkened sky. What a beautiful thing, that moon! She breathed in the smell of summer heat. The seasons in the wood were wonky, and she loved how she never knew what the weather would hold! In the distance, lightning cracked, too far away to hear the accompanying thunder. The ceremony was a simple one, requiring only the new moon and a drop of human blood upon the talismans. But Roxanne's stomach growled. She would need energy to fulfill the ritual, simple or not. Well, she could eat her meal and take the blood she needed from the stout man's body at the same time! She closed the great doors and bent down to the man on the floor inside the library. She touched his face.

"You have been good to me," she said, "despite your sex." She sunk her teeth into the only virgin skin left upon his neck and found that she had drained him dry.

Chapter Two

Panic rose into Roxanne's chest. She could not wait another month. She calculated the time it would take her to walk the tunnels into town. She could transform and fly into town, but she would not be able to take a human's blood back with her. The moon's first hour would be long passed before she returned. Roxanne slammed shut the door and frantically examined the hall with its spiderwebs in the corners. She paused. The spiderwebs were gone. They had been swept away. She searched the floor. She had seen footsteps there once or twice. She had ignored them, as she was wont to ignore things that would take too much effort to figure out. Now she realized with a start that footsteps led to feet, which led to people.

Roxanne walked the halls, her vision unimpeded by the dark. She looked for any sign of life. The halls snaked. They twisted and disappeared. She turned many times before she found what she was looking for: a single strand of hair dangling from the knob of a door. She opened the door.

On the other side, a white-haired woman dusted a bookshelf. The woman wore a black pencil skirt over a round bulb of an ass, glasses with twenty or so magnifying lenses jutting off the frames in all directions, and suspenders. She turned to face Roxanne, and Roxanne was surprised to see that she looked young—in the middle years of a human life—and that her lips were painted blue as the sky that Roxanne never got to see.

"Can I help you find something?" the woman asked.

"How long have you been here?" Roxanne stepped into the room. She pushed the door closed behind her.

"I've always been here," the woman said. She returned to her dusting.

"Are you not surprised to see me?" Roxanne advanced.

"If you think I am not apprised of everything that happens in my library, you are sorely mistaken." The woman dropped her duster on top of a row of books. She buried her hands in the pockets of her pants and faced Roxanne. "I know all about you, Roxanne. I know how you and your friends came to be here, to search the diaries of monsters past, to try to find a way to beat Lee Vansing. I know that you made a death pact to preserve your legacies, to ensure your place in history among powerful men. I know that you alone broke that pact and hid from the monster hunter, while your friends carried through. I know that you intend to bring them back. I know that you drained a man in the hall and left me quite a mess to clean. I understand that you need blood. I have a feeling you're going to try for mine."

Roxanne grinned to reveal the threat of her sharpened incisors. "You must believe that you're smart."

The woman sighed. "I am the librarian of the Great Library of Evil. I understand evil, even if I understand nothing more."

"Are you human?" Roxanne asked. "Will your blood bring back the monstrous dead?"

"More or less," the librarian said.

For a moment, the air crackled. A trumpet blew, though no one in the history of the world understood who played it or any of the music that loomed in the background.

Roxanne pounced. The librarian dodged. A drum beat.

The librarian dodged. "I'm not without my own tricks."

Roxanne pounced again. The librarian dove into a dark corner. She scurried through the shadows. Roxanne moved with enhanced speed. She jumped to join the dark. She reached out to grab the librarian's arm. Her hand wrapped around something thin and hairy. She yanked her hand into the light; she held the limb of a giant spider. She grinned, intrigued by the nature of her new foe. The limb was trying to disappear, shrinking ever smaller with the shadowed spider body attached. Roxanne cackled as she yanked the spider-woman from hiding, startling her into a return to human form. The woman's face appeared on the spider's face, and Roxanne laughed to see that the little magnifying glasses were lenses for the librarian's spider eyes. She was a clever broad! Too bad that Roxanne would not have more time to play.

As the spider's neck morphed into the woman's neck, Roxanne sank her teeth into the smooth of the librarian's skin.

Roxanne pulled back, mouth covered in blood. "I've never dined on spider before." A triumphant trumpet blared to end the song of sadism. Roxanne hoisted the half-spider, half-woman over her shoulder and carried her back to the room that housed the relics of Roxanne's dead friends.

Chapter Three

The ritual was as simple as a ritual could be: Roxanne slurped blood from the librarian's wound and spit it upon the stone head of Medusa, then the knife of Mx. Hyde. Roxanne drank the rest of the librarian's blood as she waited for the resurrections to complete.

The bodies grew slowly from nothing. Roxanne tapped her foot impatiently as she watched first the organs, then the veins, then bone, then muscle, then fat, then skin—as she watched the bodies of her friends form on the table right before her eyes. The gore was the most fascinating part, when the gooey bits melded together and the veins tried to pump, gurgling with new fluid. Toward the end of the process, Roxanne stood in wait beside the table, eager to pull Medusa and Mx. Hyde into her embrace. She watched the hair form upon their bodies. For Mx. Hyde, a mane of black in their half-and-half style: long and silky on the feminine side, and cropped in a shoulder-length bob on the masculine side. Dr. Hyde's facial features adjusted themselves accordingly: the plump feminine lips met their thin lips in the middle; their high cheekbones contrasted their flatter gaunt. The prominent chin merged into the square side. The hair down their body grew in, light and thin, and also dark and heavy.

Medusa was no less intriguing, her brown hair sprouting from her head and the snakes pushing forth from the skin of her scalp, lying as still as she lay. Their sleek black skin. Their closed eye slits. She wanted to reach out, to touch one, but stopped herself, unsure if it would affect the resurrection process.

Medusa's white dress entered the world like water poured and frozen where it touched the air, a soft nightgown of a dress with buttons down the middle and a high, frilled collar. Mx. Hyde's clothes stitched themselves upon their body: their tailored suit with half a red bowtie at the collar, half a string of pearls, the shirt half-white, half-red. The ensemble was dapper in its strange duality. They were always a sharp dresser, whereas Medusa went out in whatever she always wore, unconcerned with the way others might see her, since they could never see her eye-to-eye without losing their humanity.

"My friends," Roxanne said out loud, and as the words left her lips, the eyes of Medusa and Mx. Hyde fluttered open.

"Roxanne?" Mx. Hyde said, sitting up upon the table. "You did it!"

Roxanne embraced her friend. "I did it," Roxanne whispered.

"You intelligent creature, you," Mx. Hyde said in their familiar husk, their rotting breath caressing Roxanne's ear. They did not let go.

New arms, cloaked in loose white fabric, wrapped around them both. "It's good to be back," Medusa said in her gentle voice. "It was terrible where we were."

"Don't." Dr. Hyde shivered. "I'm not ready to talk about it yet."

Roxanne felt her friends shivering in her arms. "You're as safe as monsters here." Roxanne was the first to pull back.

"Are we still in the Great Library of Evil?" Mx. Hyde asked.

"I couldn't very well carry a stone head out of here!" Roxanne said. "We have three hours until sunrise. I've been saving the most intoxicating woman for just this occasion! She's a barmaid."

"A barmaid?" Mx. Hyde arched one eyebrow.

"Oh, she's morally bankrupt enough for you," Roxanne said. "I sense her filth."

Mx. Hyde raised the second eyebrow. "I'm open-minded."

"And for you, M, there are stupid men aplenty in town. I've been feeding off the population for a full month, and still they frequent the local tavern."

Medusa sighed happily. "They sound dreamy. There were no men down there. Well, there was one—"

Dr. Hyde shushed her. "He is not a man," they said. "And I said I didn't want to talk about it."

Silence settled. It made Roxanne uncomfortable. They were supposed to be celebrating! There was maiming to do.

"Shall we?" Roxanne offered her looped arms. Mx. Hyde and Medusa threaded their elbows through and giggled as they kissed both of her pale cheeks.

Reunited at last, the Monsters Three made their way through the library, past Roxanne's rotting man, and down a trap door that led to the most direct tunnel into town. With her friends present for company, Roxanne wasn't bothered by the mosquitos. Dr. Hyde caught one in their hand and pinched off the creature's wings. They pocketed the wriggling body. Roxanne and Medusa teased them about their constant surveillance of the world and led Mx. Hyde along the path. Unlike Roxanne and Medusa, the doctor could not see in the dark.

In town, the Monsters Three strode through the tavern doors. But the evening was late, and only a single man snoozed at a tavern table while the owner sloshed water over the dirtied floor.

"Closing up, ladies," the owner said. "I can give you a cup of mead if you'd like to down it in one go. Or three little cakes, if you looking for something sweet. My cook made them this morning, and I'm afraid it's the only foodstuff we have left tonight."

Roxanne's stomach flipped. "The barmaid?"

"You mean Deenie?" The half-smile that crossed his face told Roxanne that was exactly who she meant. "She's likely found her fun elsewhere by now. She never stays here long, that Deenie."

"Where has she gone?" Roxanne said.

"There's no telling," he said. "I'll let her know you're looking for her. What do I call you?"

Roxanne scanned her surroundings. Well, she would take what she could get. She shared a knowing glance with Medusa, who moved to the only challenge in the room: the sleeping man, whose eyes seemed glued shut. Roxanne swept forward across the room and jerked the owner's head to one side while she sunk her teeth into the other.

"You will call me death," she whispered into his ear, then let his body fall.

Mx. Hyde pursed their lips and buried their hands in their pockets. "The mosquito was more exciting."

Roxanne wiped her mouth and frowned. "I'd like to stop feasting on men, really I would."

"Looks to be a pattern with you since we were offed," Mx. Hyde said. "Following in M's footsteps?"

Roxanne and Mx. Hyde turned to face Medusa, who now sat in the chair next to the drunkard, speaking sweet nothings into his slumbering ear. He did not stir. She shook him. He snored on. She forced one of his eyes open, then the other, and tried to look into them, but his pupils hid. She rested her own head on the table.

"A failure on all fronts," Roxanne said as blood pooled from the bar owner's throat around her shoes.

Mx. Hyde rested their hand on Roxanne's shoulder. "I'll be fine. M will survive, too. We've gone longer." They stepped clear of the blood puddle. "We might as well head back, get some rest. Travel on to somewhere more exciting once night falls again."

Roxanne stomped her foot, and the bar rattled. "This was supposed to be a celebration!" she cried. She swept her arm along the bar and sent a wave of dirty glasses tumbling and breaking in her midst.

"Come now," Mx. Hyde said. "Rest is for the wicked."

The man beside Medusa sat up. "I'll clean it up! No need to nag!" His sleepy eyelids fluttered open.

"You'd better," M said, and when the man looked at her, she caught his eye. Her snakes broke free of her curls and danced their terrible choreography. He could not look away. His body crackled as it turned to stone. M smiled her sad smile and stood from the table. "Another weak one," she said, remembering the man she'd loved before her death, the man whom she had killed for love. He had been able to look into her eyes, the only man she'd met who could.

"Well, see there, M got a decent meal! Not a total failure." Mx. Hyde bumped Roxanne beneath her chin. "Tomorrow will be a better night."

Medusa held Roxanne's hand as they walked from the bar. "Thanks for bringing us back," she said.

"Thanks for coming back," Roxanne said as the dark sky swallowed their shadows from the cobblestone streets.

In the room where Roxanne had brought her friends back to life, light crept in through the lonely high window. Roxanne felt her body shutting down despite her desire to remain awake. She yawned.

"You performed a difficult task." Dr. Hyde wrapped one arm around Roxanne's shoulder. "Where is your coffin? You need your rest."

"But you only just returned—" Roxanne tried to argue, but Mx. Hyde searched the room.

"Oh, you dear," Medusa said. "Where is your nest?"

"I've been nesting in the stacks." Roxanne gestured vaguely.

"We'll get you a proper coffin tomorrow," Medusa said. She smoothed her white dress across her lap. "Perhaps we can raid the coffin maker's shop! Rent a proper horse and carriage, find a big lair out in the hills!"

Mx. Hyde and Roxanne shared a look, then laughed. "Medusa and her big dreams!" Roxanne said as she sunk to the floor and slithered into the stacks. "Oh, Hyde, I forgot! There's a body in the corner, a woman. The librarian. You can feed on her!" She yawned again, falling into her oblivion. As she drifted away, she heard the voices of her friends.

"There's no woman here," Dr. Hyde said as they searched the room.

"Will you be okay? You won't transform into Jekyll alone without the extraction?" Medusa said.

"I need it less and less." Mx. Hyde said.

"I feel just like I've never slept a day in my life," Medusa said. "But death is like sleep, is it not? We should feel more well-rested."

"No, the processes are altogether different." Mx. Hyde collapsed into a dark corner.

Medusa slunk slowly to the ground beside them. "I'm a bit afraid to sleep again. I'm a bit afraid I'll die."

Mx. Hyde reached out their hand, and one of Medusa's snakes broke forth and wrapped sleepily around their hand. Medusa let her eyes close, and Mx. Hyde followed suit, and the deep breaths of the Monsters Three were like the softest of songs in the dark.

And Roxanne closed her eyes and slept the sleep of the living dead.

❖

It was the day they had met: Mx. Hyde studied the hundreds of stone statues in the mansion courtyard, mossy and cracked and home to all manner of bugs. They wanted to study the creatures—here especially, in this dream of that night, they were fascinated by species they had never before glimpsed—but more than that, they wanted to study the creature who was rumored to live within the rundown mansion. Ever since Mx. Hyde discovered the formula for womanhood, a formula whose secret ingredient was a hormone found in only the female body, they had longed to discover a source powerful enough to last forever. It was dreary to kill a new woman every other evening, and the bodies were increasingly difficult with which to deal. Never mind the other issues: that Mx. Hyde was at war with themself, that the Hyde and the Jekyll would not come to an agreement for the sharing of one body. Those were problems for another time. This night, the night the Monsters Three met for the first time, Hyde desired to solve the problem of longevity, for the woman who owned the rundown mansion was said to be as ancient as womankind.

But Dr. Hyde had misidentified her; Dr. Hyde had been stalking Roxanne.

Mx. Hyde padded through the courtyard. Despite their carefulness, leaves crunched beneath their feet. They winced with each sound. Around the courtyard, every flower was dead. The air smelled of decay. Mx. Hyde thumbed at the knife in their pocket; they felt one with its sharp eagerness to sink into a woman's throat.

Ahead, a shadow moved across the courtyard.

Hyde lunged toward it. They landed on their hands and knees. Their kneecaps stung. A woman cackled. The noise sent a shiver down Mx. Hyde's spine.

They followed the sound until they arrived at a door broken into two pieces. They stepped through and into the half-abandoned mansion. Leaves blew across the

concrete with each breath of the wind through the broken windows. Hyde avoided the shards of glass on the
floor, but no longer for the sound; they had given in to
the idea that their victim knew they were coming for her.

Roxanne knew. Roxanne had heard the horses' hoof-
beats from Hyde's carriage. She'd been exploring the mansion. Roxanne loved a good mansion with its labyrin-
thine hallways. She loved chasing women through them,
cornering women in an old room crowded with ancient
furniture. This one, Mx. Hyde, was curious and fearless.
It thrilled Roxanne.

Roxanne led her prey through hallway after hallway,
winding them around staircases and through roach-in-
fested crevices, around errant statues that blocked the
way. She frowned at the path. Had it been this way before? Time had weathered her memories of the night she
first met M and Mx. Hyde, but she had recalled accurate-
ly adventures far older than this. Had she really led Hyde
through such a large number of rooms? There were too
many bedrooms to count.

Finally, Roxanne arrived in the room of ghosts. She
had taken to calling it that in her recollections, and she
thought it now as she swept around the chaise draped in
spidery white cloth and stood her ground, still as a statue,
beside a vanity. She pulled the sheet away from it. The
cloth withered to the ground, disturbing the dust where
it landed and creating a cloud that coated Roxanne's sig-
nature red dress. Her reflection failed to register in the
vanity's cracked mirror. There, like a statue, she waited
for Mx. Hyde to enter her trap.

Out of the three of them, Medusa loved visitors the
most. For twenty long years, she had wandered her halls,
lonely but for the scavengers who came to steal old valu-
ables or adventurers curious about the legend of the ghost
woman who dwelled within the old mansion. Medusa en-

tered the room to find Roxanne and Mx. Hyde face-to-face, daring one another to strike first. Medusa grinned as her snakes broke free from her hair and swayed about her head.

Roxanne hissed, baring her fangs. Mx. Hyde turned, then jumped back. They knocked into Roxanne. The two grabbed onto one another in an effort to maintain their balance. They both looked straight at Medusa and remained skin-and-bone.

"Your hair is amazing," Roxanne said. She stepped around Mx. Hyde, toward Medusa, and reached out to pet a snake.

"I wouldn't—" Medusa began, but the snake struck the fatty round of Roxanne's thumb before the words left her mouth.

Roxanne cackled. "What a vicious garment."

"It's not a garment," Medusa said. Her voice was strange; strangled, not at all like it had been that night. "It's me."

Mx. Hyde stepped forward beside Roxanne. "What are you?" they said.

"What are you?" Medusa said, and despite her strangled throat, Hyde understood her.

"I'm a doctor."

"Me too," Roxanne said. "I'm a doctor too."

"You're a vampire," Medusa tried to say, as she had in the true moment, she knew she had, but now her voice was obstructed. She could not breathe. She clutched at her stomach and gagged. She fell to the floor. Her friends did not rush to help but stood and watched. They would have helped her! But it didn't happen like this. The memory changed in front of them, morphing into nightmare.

She hacked until the snake in her throat slithered free and slid across the floor.

"Is that normal for your kind?" Mx. Hyde said, and Medusa shook her head, still stunned. Then another snake crawled forth from her mouth, then another, then another. "Are you sure this isn't a common occurrence?" Hyde said, but even as they said it, they knew it wasn't common. They knew, in the pit of their stomach, that Medusa had been their friend for many years and had never, in all that time, vomited snakes.

Medusa heaved again and again. The room was filling fast, a layer of snakes sliding across the floor, crawling all over her body and nipping at the feet of Roxanne and Hyde, who had to stomp them away when they tried to slither upward. Then came a sharp pain in her throat, and another, but no, this was not a snake. This object cut at her like splinters, and from her mouth protruded the tip of a cane, or so it seemed as she tried to grab it and pull.

Roxanne rushed to help. She pulled at the wooden stick while Mx. Hyde kicked the relentless snakes to form a small island of cleared space in the middle of the floor. Roxanne yanked at the stick in one final gesture. It broke free. At its other end, the stick was flat and wide and covered in blood: an oar. Medusa spat blood onto the floor, her throat ravaged.

"Where the hell did that come from?" Roxanne said, and then she felt a hand close around its other end.

"I'll take that." The man wrested the oar from Roxanne with one strong pull. His arrival coincided with the whine of a theremin. His hands had claws that looked like sharpened rib bones. He wore a robe made of mist that obscured the shape of his body. He hunched forward. They could not see his face.

"Is it yours?" Roxanne said. "What was it doing in our friend's throat?"

"Friends, are you?" the man said. "You've only just met."

Roxanne's brain fogged. They had only just met—and yet she understood, as in a dream, that they were friends and had been beyond this night.

"No," Medusa croaked.

"That isn't true," Roxanne said. "We take care of one another."

"Not you," Medusa said. Blood coated her lips.

Hyde glanced up from the snakes. They honed in on the man and shook their head as memory returned to them. "It's you."

"You know this man?" Roxanne squared her shoulders and formed a wall of her body beside Medusa.

"The guardian." Mx. Hyde reached forward and wrapped their hand around Roxanne's forearm.

"Yes, they know me," he said. "And I know you, Roxanne. The Vampire Queen. The Vampire Lover. Oh, you have many names, Roxanne, in the underworld." He struck his oar against the floor. "The Vampire Battleax. The Vampire Wench. My favorite: the Vampire Harpy. For you are a harpy, Roxanne. You take what does not belong to you." The man lunged forward and disappeared in a cloud of mist then reappeared behind Roxanne and wrapped one hand around her throat. He rammed his oar at her back, at the space that hid her heart, but she ducked before it struck. The tip nicked Hyde's arm, and as he yanked it free, blood poured from the wound. Hyde held their arm to their chest to slow the bleeding. On the floor, Medusa struggled to squirm away, but her palms slipped upon the snakes' slick skins. Her face smacked the marble floor.

"And what do they call you?" Roxanne balanced, crouched, on the front of her red heels.

"They call me many names as well." He readjusted his cloak. He paced in front of them. As he moved, a hundred skulls formed a misty train behind him. "You may have heard of some—"

Roxanne hoisted Medusa over her shoulder, stood, and sprinted through the snakes. Her heels dug into the reptiles, grinding them into the floor. Blood gathered on her feet. Roxanne hoped that Hyde had followed suit, but she could not stop to make sure—and the doctor had always been decent at taking care of themself. Roxanne burst through a door and sprinted through the halls until she came to a door half-propped open. She crossed the threshold and fell down and down, clinging to Medusa's body, deafened by Medusa's screaming in her ear.

Chapter Four

Roxanne landed with a cracking of her bones. Medusa tumbled from her shoulders and sprawled across the ground. Roxanne stood and tried to run a hand down her dress—but the dress was gone. She stared at her naked body. She ran her hand down her curves, then laughed.

"Medusa, we've got to wake up." She bent again. She shook her friend.

"What are you doing?" Medusa cried out, but Roxanne only shook harder.

"Wake up!" Roxanne yelled, and with a start, Roxanne woke.

Medusa and Mx. Hyde writhed on the floor in their sleep. Roxanne crawled across the floor and shook Medusa free from her nightmare. Once Medusa's eyes fluttered open, Roxanne screeched into Hyde's ear. Hyde sat upright. Blood gushed from their arm. Medusa coughed blood into her hand. Only Roxanne had awoken unscathed.

"Who the hell was that?" Roxanne pressed her hands to Dr. Hyde's wound. She tried not to take too deep a breath of the fresh blood, tried not to look at its ruby slickness. "What do I do?"

"M, tear me some cloth," Hyde said.

Medusa ripped the bottom of her dress with her teeth and pulled a strip of cloth from the garment.

"Now tie it around my upper arm, to slow the bleeding!"

Medusa did as she was told. The bleeding slowed.

"Move away now," Mx. Hyde said.

"But you're still—"

"And you love a midnight snack. Move away now!" Hyde said.

Roxanne scurried into the shadows. "Who was that?" she repeated.

"M, I need you to gather some string and one of my needles, anything you can use to stitch me up." Mx. Hyde held their arm across their chest and grimaced. "You asked me, Roxanne, who that man was? That man was the guardian of the underworld. Out there, in that world, he was our Master. We were his servants."

Medusa searched the library shelves at a frantic pace.

"What does he want?" Roxanne asked.

Medusa shrugged, then grimaced again. "No clue."

Roxanne paced. Medusa gathered a clump of old spiderweb and presented it to Hyde.

"It will do," Hyde said, pulling it taught to test the strength. "And my needle?"

Medusa searched the shelves for the syringe materials that Hyde had hidden when they first arrived in this place.

"Well, whatever he wants, he's mad as hell about it," Roxanne said.

"I'd imagine so," Hyde said.

Medusa found them lying in the dust. Mx. Hyde nodded as Medusa bent the needle into a half-circle and prepared the spiderwebbing to pass through the hollow core.

"You can't be here for this," Hyde said.

"I'm fine." Roxanne furrowed her brows. "You think I can't handle myself?"

"You cannot," Medusa said as she knelt beside Mx. Hyde. "We know you cannot."

Roxanne's skin felt hot—her whole body burned. She wanted to argue, but she understood that there was indeed a time and a place and that this was neither. They were wrong. She could handle herself fine, but she would do as Hyde asked and leave the room. But she couldn't just wait outside the door. She had to do something, to make it right.

"That's all fine." She stomped out of the room and let the door slam. She stomped through the entryway, past the decaying man, stopping only briefly to take in the sweet putrefaction. She stomped through the front doors and into the garden. A fine mist lay across the ground. Mosquitos formed a cloud in the humid air. Roxanne waded through them and into the depths of the garden where she had glimpsed the sleeping belles. She plucked the purple bean pods, enough to take down a horse, then three pods more.

"I didn't save my friends only to have them chased by some madman," she muttered through her full mouth as she chewed through the bean pods' bitter skin.

She felt the effects at once: her body shutting down as it had during her very first death. Her vision a pinpoint of bright. Her head light with loss. Falling. The grass soft and wet. The fog a blanket. The brain busy with memory.

Roxanne danced in a white dress. She had dreamt of the night she became a vampire so many times that she no longer knew which details had been real and which she had, over the years, embellished, but the white dress was a constant. As was her constant attention for one person in the room: her friend, her beauty, her Belle. Roxanne was happy for the striped cat mask that obscured her eyes, for as she danced with every man at the masquerade, her gaze never left her Belle.

The aristocrat in the purple cape did not care if Roxanne looked at him or not. None of the old men did; they were happy to be seen with such young flowers. This one grinned stupidly with his bad teeth. That one moved like his feet were broken. This one stopped and clutched his heart. Roxanne's gaze left Belle for the first time all night.

"Are you all right?" she asked, holding the man up as best as she could.

"I can't breathe," he wheezed. "Take me outside."

"Of course." Roxanne led the man from the floor, panic rising inside her.

Once outside, he stood straight again. Roxanne remembered: he removed his mask, revealed his teeth, and ripped the neck of her dress. He sunk his teeth into her. She faded. That was how it went, both in reality and in every dream she dreamt since.

He removed his mask. He revealed his sharp front teeth.

He removed his mask. He dealt Roxanne her death.

He removed his mask. He wore two copper coins over his eyes. The skin sagged off his bones.

Roxanne screamed. His purple cloak spread like mist on the ground, and in his right hand, he held his long oar. He reached out with his claws of sharpened bone and struck her once across her face. She fell back. Not her face. Anything but her face. She pressed her hands to her cheeks. She felt five gashes thick with gore. She screamed again.

"You stole from me, Roxanne," the guardian said. He thrust forward the pointed end of his oar. It stuck her in the neck. She gasped, stuck like meat on a skewer, and he yanked the oar from her flesh.

She struggled to her hands and knees, then to her feet, scurrying away from him all the while. When finally she stood, she turned and ran across the muddy street parked with carriages, down the steep hill that led to a river. She stopped at the river's edge. Running water. It was dangerous to a vampire, but she was not yet a vampire, not in this dream, this memory that had been tampered with. She stuck her toes into the water. Her skin hissed and burned, and her white slipper fell from her foot now slick with pain.

Up on the hilltop, the guardian laughed. His laugh sounded like boiling blood.

Roxanne limped along the river. The guardian began his descent, each step slower than the last. Still, he gained on her. He was behind her. He grabbed her by the shoulder and held her where she stood. She could not move. She closed her eyes and waited for death. She opened her eyes. She lay in the fog outside the Great Library of Evil. Still paralyzed. She closed her eyes. His breath blew hot upon her neck.

"You know you cannot get away from me," he said.

"What do you want?" she said. And he ripped into her neck with his claws and tore out her flesh, and she wilted to the ground.

Roxanne woke in a hedge maze, the very same from her past. The guardian sat on a severed stump beside her. This was right; in her past, the aristocrat had taken her to the hedge maze and allowed her to wake as a vampire trapped. He had told her that they would live together forever, which was when she murdered him with a sharpened branch and grinned with her new sharp smile as he bled then turned to ash before her eyes.

Now, she could not escape with the help of a sharpened branch. She did not know what the guardian was, but he was no vampire. She ached all over. Her neck was a gaping wound she could not stand to inspect. Instead she studied his hunched form.

"Can you explain any of this to me?" she said.

He leaned forward, resting his head in his hand. "Roxanne, do you understand balance?" he said. "Do you understand delicate ecosystems?"

"No," Roxanne said.

"I thought not," he said. "You took two deliciously evil creatures from my underworld. You changed the landscape when I was not yet ready for it to be changed. How can a man plan anything when he is not in charge of what goes on in his own world?"

Roxanne removed her shredded slippers and tossed them into a bramble. "Do I care?" she said. "You're talking about the resurrection? You're mad that I brought my friends back."

"I'm mad that you brought your friends back," he said.

"You mean to kill them again?"

"And you," he said. "I would love to see you suffer."

Roxanne rolled her eyes, though in her chest, her dead heart did tremble. She was not used to being afraid.

The guardian stood and paced. "This is quite fun for me." He studied his long claws, flexed and unflexed them. "I think I'll tear you apart strip by strip. You don't bleed much, vampires, when you haven't fed—and I like the idea of a bloodless mess of vampire gore."

The remainder of this memory was a good one, and Roxanne had revisited it enough times to recall the path out of the maze. After emerging from the hedges, she had knocked at the door of the nearby manor. She drained the servant girl. She crept upstairs and drained the parents in the bed. She fell asleep beside the young woman, her own age, and woke to her screaming. She drained that woman too. Her first tastes of blood. Inflicting terror was intoxicating, and Roxanne would not let this man take her un-death away from her.

"Let's make a bargain," she said.

"A bargain?" He stopped.

"You like bargains. I know that much about the under-world. I know that much about evil. It's all games with us. Games, and suffering." She fought to her feet, and every movement sent a terrible shock through her body. "Play games with us. Make us suffer."

The mist cleared from around the guardian. "You aren't wrong. I like games."

"I knew it," Roxanne said.

The guardian scratched at his chin. A hunk of skin peeled off under his fingernail. He flicked it away. "Your debt to me is three monsters, Roxanne. If you can send me three monsters, I may find your debt repaid."

"I took two from you," Roxanne said. "And may isn't strong enough."

"Are you in a position to argue?" He gestured at the stinging wound in her neck. His acknowledgment made it hurt. She did not mind hurt, but she preferred to inflict it rather than receive it.

"We'll get you two monsters," she said.

He lunged forward, swift as a sudden storm, and buried his claws in her ruined flesh. Roxanne fell again to the ground, her vision a white screen.

"Fine!" she yelled. "Three monsters!"

"Balance needs to be maintained, Roxanne. I need re-placements, you see: for the life of Mx. Hyde, for Medusa, for the Great Librarian." He twisted his bone claw, and it nudged through her muscle and clinked against her own bone.

The pain seared through her. "The librarian?"

"Yes. Now, I know it's not your fault that she, of all peo-ple, was resurrected. But it is your fault that she arrived in my underworld at all. I don't like to have things taken away, and I don't much care whose fault it is." His breath smelled like necrosis; it was a wonderful smell, and Rox-anne wished that she could enjoy it. "It's funny, Roxanne, but the only reason I am able to meet you here like this? It was her blood that opened the way. Her blood that brought us together.

"But no matter. My underworld is a mess with all this resurrection. Without balance, Roxanne, the underworld is chaos. I do not like chaos."

"I understand," she said in a whisper.

"I don't think you do." He kneeled against her leg. "Three monsters are all I need from you, Roxanne. And I have a perfect three in mind." With his other hand, he cut a slit in the belly of her dress. He carved into her skin. "But I don't want excess stock, you understand. Send me more than three innocent creatures, more than three people for which I did not ask, the deal is off." It was a name he was carving into her. Roxanne gritted her sharpened teeth, her fangs tearing apart her lips. "If you send me more than three innocent creatures before you've satisfied our terms, I will kill your friends, then you, and I will make it slow." It was three names he carved, but she could not read them, skewered as she was. "I will make it painful."

"But we can't survive without feeding," she said.

"You have until the next new moon." He removed his claws from her skin. She rolled over and tried not to cry. "I love a good deadline!" He rubbed his hands together, and his claws clanked against one another. He turned then and crept away through the hedge maze, the skulls stretching out in an endless mist behind him as he moved. As he neared the end of Roxanne's sightline, he pulled his hood back over his rotting face.

Roxanne lay in the dirt, the pain in her neck white hot, the names screaming on her abdomen. She crawled to the edge of the nearest hedge and tried to claw at the brambles, but the shrub gored her knuckles. She needed blood, but more than that, she needed to be inside of the manor before the sun rose. The pink dawn threatened.

She tore through the hedge with animal ferocity, opening a small escape. She crawled through. The hedge tore at her clothes. She arrived at another hedge. She clawed her way through. Then another. And another, until Roxanne emerged into the courtyard she had once run through in the dark of night, then again and again in her sweetest dreams. Now the courtyard was bright with morning. She stared down the sun, and it ate into her. She felt her body shake.

Chapter Five

Roxanne opened her eyes to the face of her friend. Medusa shook her vigorously.

"You're a damn fool," Hyde said from above them, but Medusa leaned down to embrace Roxanne. Roxanne cried out.

"You're wounded!" Medusa pulled back and examined Roxanne's body through the mist. She pursed her lips when she saw the neck wound, but she traced the bloodless edge of the carvings upon Roxanne's stomach. "What are these?"

"Victims," Roxanne said. "Our new enemies."

"Needleskin. Zeeka. Hector." Dr. Hyde frowned. "I've never heard of these people."

"I'll explain everything," Roxanne said. Her voice had never sounded so weak, not even when she was a shy human striving to impress her sweetest friend. "Get me inside."

After Medusa carried Roxanne back to her nest, Hyde worried over Roxanne's withered body. They instructed Medusa in the right night garden herbs to pick then grind with her teeth and spit to create a healing paste. They instructed Medusa in how thick to apply the paste upon Roxanne's neck. As she spread it on the wound, Roxanne told her friends about her encounter with the Guardian and the deal she had made.

"These are the monsters we're to kill." Roxanne gestured toward her belly.

"We don't kill monsters," Medusa said as she wiped her hands against the stone wall. "It's rude."

"You don't have to do anything," Roxanne said. "I'll take care of everything, and as quickly as I can. But there's a catch: we can't kill more than three extraneous people, three 'innocent' people, until I succeed."

"Excuse me?" Dr. Hyde said.

"Surely you have a surplus hidden away, back in your old apartment, perhaps?" Medusa said.

"If that place hasn't been raided to hell," Dr. Hyde said.

"Roxanne, you cannot be serious. There's no way you can do this alone. If these monsters are as terrible as we are—"

"We're quite good," Dr. Hyde said. "Not easily replaceable, you know."

Roxanne smiled despite herself. "Of course not. But I made this deal."

"Because you brought us back from death," Medusa said.

Dr. Hyde shrugged. "I'll do whatever you two do. We're a team."

"Even if I'm a bloodthirsty vampire?" Roxanne said.

Dr. Hyde shrugged. "Listen, we all have flaws."

"Stop this!" Medusa said. "You're both bleeding out—er, gaping out—and still snapping at one another, however playfully you claim it is! We've been through worse than this. We've fought great monster hunters. We've outshined Dracula. We've taken out whole towns, whole families, and dealt with mobs of angry people."

"Taking on three monsters may be a whole other level of challenge, Roxanne," Dr. Hyde said. "I'm up for it. But we need to prepare ourselves."

"These names," Medusa said. "How are we to decode these names?"

Mx. Hyde placed their hands on their hips. "I wonder where we could possibly find information on monsters."

Medusa looked up and around. Roxanne groaned.

"I'll start," Hyde said. "Here with the autobiographies seems an easy place."

While Roxanne rested, thankful that she healed quickly even for a monster, Mx. Hyde and Medusa scoured the author names. "Needleskin, needleskin, needleskin," Medusa said, tracing the book spines. "No Needleskin in the Ns, I'm afraid." They searched each spine, in case the names were first names, and rooted out a single Hector. They uncovered no Zeeka, and as they flipped through the Hector, they doubted that he could be the monster that the Guardian desired: Hector was a mere ghost and incapable of anything more than small pranks that he wrote about in long-winded detail.

After many hours of scanning, they settled on the floor for a fearful sleep, but exhaustion finally overtook them, and they were not plagued by nightmares. By the next evening, Roxanne had nearly healed, the carvings but pencil scratches, and Mx. Hyde had regained a bounce in their step.

"Ready to read?" Mx. Hyde prodded Roxanne with their elbow as they stood to dress and face the night.

"Fine," Roxanne said, and the Monsters Three moved on to the next room within the Great Library of Evil.

It took precisely one hour for Roxanne to grow too bored to continue.

"You two are better at it than me!" She lay down on the floor. "I'm only crowding your way."

"And what exactly will you do instead?" Mx. Hyde said. They had discovered a section labeled HISTORY OF MONSTROSITY, and they sat at a half-broken desk paging through a volume's index in the light from a gas lamp. "Pout? Moan? Annoy us?"

"Yes," Roxanne said. "Those things sound far superior!"

Mx. Hyde and Medusa rolled their eyes in tandem, but three hours later, once Roxanne had sighed one too many times, Mx. Hyde threw down their book.

"And how do you suggest we find these monsters?" they said.

Roxanne started to shrug, but then she half-remembered something from her dream; it crept back, something about the library—like clearing away spider webbing, she thought, uncovering information from dreams—and then she sat straight up. "Spiders!" she said. "The Guardian said that the Great Librarian of Evil returned from death!" Roxanne cursed herself. It was the whole reason he claimed he needed three monsters, not two. "She might know where to find info. She's the archivist, after all. Got her nose in all these moldy books."

"They're not moldy," Medusa said.

"Where does this Great Librarian dwell?" Mx. Hyde asked, shutting the book they were perusing with umph.

Roxanne sprang to her feet. "Last time, I followed her footprints."

"A true detective," Mx. Hyde said.

Roxanne held open the creaking door for her friends.

"A true gentleperson," Mx. Hyde said, bowing a little as they exited the room.

Together, the Monsters Three searched the halls for footprints, but the floor was clean as a room wiped of evidence. Roxanne wrapped her hand around each doorknob that they passed, hoping to find the sticky spiderwebbing that had first led her to the Great Librarian, but the doorknobs were clean too.

"Back to reading," Mx. Hyde said with a sigh, but Roxanne grinned her terrible grin.

"I have an idea." She barged into the nearest room labeled SOUNDTRACKS TO TERROR and filled with sheet music carefully filed into black folios. Roxanne yanked free the folio nearest to her and scattered the sheet music across the floor.

"Oh, destruction!" Medusa said, pulling a folio from a shelf.

One-half of Hyde's face smiled, while the other frowned. "But—" they started to say before they silenced themself. They kicked the paper as they meandered to a shelf and yanked the whole thing down on top of them. They laughed as the shelf cracked across their chest. Roxanne and Medusa paused only a moment before they continued their reign of mess.

Roxanne had assumed that the Great Librarian would come running, but perhaps a mess was not enough for her to risk it. Roxanne whipped free a sheet and ripped it in half.

The door flew closed, and the Great Librarian stood before them. "What do you think you're doing?" she said.

Roxanne let the paper halves flutter to the floor. "Lovely to see you again, Librarian."

"You've violated my only rule, vampire." The librarian pointed to a plaque upon the wall; Roxanne could almost swear it hadn't been there before: DO NOT DESTROY THE BOOKS, it read.

"Oops," Roxanne said.

Mx. Hyde stepped between the librarian and Roxanne. "We need some information," they said. "We only want your help. Your expertise."

"You could have just rung the bell," the librarian said.

"What bell?" Medusa said.

"The bell at the front of the library," the librarian said. "Are you all oblivious to the world around you, or is it just this one?" She gestured at Roxanne.

"You're just mad because I killed you," Roxanne said.

"I got over it well enough." The librarian stuck her thumbs under her suspenders and snapped them.

"You killed her?" Medusa said.

"I assure you, I am quite intelligent," Mx. Hyde said.

"Anyway," the librarian said, pursing her lips, "what was it you're looking for? I'm very busy, you know."

"We're looking for monsters," Mx. Hyde said.

"Look in a mirror as of late?" the librarian said, but Mx. Hyde was unfazed.

"Needleskin. Zeeka. Hector." Mx. Hyde nodded curtly. "Have you heard of them?"

"Hector, I've heard of." The librarian turned, opened the door, and gestured to the Monsters Three to follow her through. As they walked through the halls, lamps along the wall lit their way. Upon closer inspection, the lamps were spun sacs filled with light. Finally, they arrived at a door labeled TITILLATING STORIES WITH AN ELEMENT OF TRUTH.

"My favorite room," the librarian said as she opened the door, but inside it looked like every other room. "These books are the most fun to read." The librarian scanned the spines until she found what she was looking for: A FAILED EXORCISM, the title read.

"It was written by a psychologist," the librarian said, handing over the text. "A case study, with elements of fiction for excitement's sake, about the young man Hector, whose body is inhabited by a demon. The psychologist fails to exorcise the demon but instead teaches them to share one body." The librarian ran her finger along her lip. "There's some lascivious stuff in there once the man grows into a proper adult."

Medusa snatched the book from Mx. Hyde's grasp. "I'll hold onto this one."

"Does it say where they're located?" Roxanne asked. "That's really all we need to know."

"Oh, this is local history," she said. "He lives in his family's manor near the Cherry Orchard. Right outside Brightleaf."

"Lovely, thank you," Medusa said softly.

"And the others?" Mx. Hyde said.

The librarian raised her eyebrows. "Needleskin? Zeeka?" She giggled. "I haven't the faintest. But do you know what's even wiser than knowing all there is to know in the world? Understanding that it is sometimes necessary to ask for assistance. Follow me."

"Again?" Roxanne said, but Hyde and Medusa followed at once, and Roxanne took her place as caboose.

The Great Librarian led them down more hallways that looked the same as the last hallways, until they came to a large open space with a giant skylight. Roxanne approached slowly, but there was no sun to be seen. In the middle of the open space, a fountain shaped like a kraken taking down a ship bubbled, and from each of the creature's tentacles, webbing stretched to the ceiling.

"Inquiry: Needleskin." The librarian stood before the fountain. "Second inquiry: Zeeka." She giggled again.

All at once, spiders emerged from the shadows and crawled across the webbing to the floor, where they formed a massive writhing pile. They convened in a mass of black, then scattered, skittering across the floor in all directions.

"What was that?" Roxanne said.

"Are they . . . trained spiders?" Mx. Hyde said.

"They are indeed," the librarian said.

Medusa said nothing, as she had taken a seat upon the floor and was nose-deep in A FAILED EXORCISM, scanning the text for the naughty bits.

A clutter of spiders returned carrying two books upon their backs. The librarian gathered the books and read the titles: *A Living History of Hedons*, the sight of which made her skin brighten, and *Experiments of Zeeka, Volume 1*. She passed *Living History* to Roxanne and *Experiments* to Mx. Hyde.

"That guardian is a cheeky man," the librarian said.

Roxanne frowned. "What do you mean?"

Mx. Hyde opened her book to the author's notes at the end. "I am a scientist living in an underground laboratory. These are my first experiments with the art of transmogrification," they read aloud. They frowned. "These monsters were clearly chosen to reflect our own interests."

"He wants to cloud your judgment when you meet them," the librarian said. "Make you think you could be friends instead."

Roxanne considered the eager scanning of their friend Medusa. "Or lovers."

"As it were," the librarian said. "Best be careful, and clear-headed."

"Thanks, mother," Roxanne said, opening her own book to a blank page at the end. "This one's not finished." She flipped to the front of the book; only a handful of pages had been printed on.

"This one's part of the living history series," the librarian said. "It populates as the events unfold. Looks like your monster here is relatively new, considering."

"Ugh." Roxanne slammed the book shut. "Newly minted monsters are the worst. They have all those grand ideas."

Mx. Hyde cackled. "Destroying the world!"

"Killing all the humans," Roxanne said.

"Cataloguing every dark thing that creeps," the librarian said, then shrugged. "I've accomplished that one. Not a layabout like you lot."

"Falling in love." Medusa sighed and shut her own book, returning to the conversation as though she had fallen free from a trance. "That's all I ever wanted, you know?"

"We know," Roxanne said, and she bent down to embrace her friend. Hyde placed a palm upon the back of Roxanne's dress. The spiders skittered back to their web, and from the corner of her eye, Medusa saw the librarian smile. "You can get in here, librarian," Roxanne said.

But the librarian only crossed her arms across her chest. "It's okay. I prefer to watch."

Chapter Six

After perusing *Living History* in the room that Roxanne had learned, over the last month, to call her own, Roxanne grew even more frustrated.

"There's nothing here about location," she said.

All that the book contained was a story about a young woman who loved to stay out at night, who sought out big men in the tavern where she worked and followed them home. How she tied them up, then teased them with the tip of a blade, how she let them bite bloody marks into her skin, how she drank and smoked opium and grew bored with the day and bored with the night. How she met a man who grew tired of entertaining her and shoved a wooden puzzle box into her hands. "If you're so bored, figure this out," he said as he disappeared into his work, "or else leave, go home. You do have a home, don't you?"

She did not have a home: just a tavern where she served and the beds of many men and women, who served her.

She struggled at the puzzle for a long while, until she finally asked the man for his help.

"I've never solved it," he said. "I was hoping you would."

She bid him goodbye, but before she went, she slipped the puzzle box into her pocket. She didn't understand why she felt the urge to steal it, beyond that it vexed her—and she was not one to be vexed. In a way she hated the box for taking away her boredom; it had become a part of her, as much as her silky curls and the corset that she tied tightly to cut off her own breath.

In her breaks at the tavern, during the hours when everyone else slept, she worried at the puzzle.

It was her blood that finally opened it: a drip from a wound from an old scab torn off when she scrubbed her hands too hard at the mudroom sink of her employer's house. The box vibrated in her hand. It tickled her skin. She giggled as the box unfolded against her, as it emitted strange blue light from every crack. The light overtook the room where she stood. It overtook her, and suddenly, she found herself in a world made of stone walls that formed a labyrinth stretching out in front of her.

At the end of the labyrinth, she met a host of creatures. They ate her up. They spat her out. They made her one of them. They set her loose upon the world.

Roxanne read the pages to Medusa and Mx. Hyde.

"Sounds like your crush at the tavern," Mx. Hyde said.

Roxanne frowned. "No," she said. "Couldn't be." She read back over the brief description of the woman in the text. "That would be a huge coincidence."

"This monster life? It's full of coincidence," Dr. Hyde said "Slumber party's over, M!"

Medusa sighed. "It was fun while it lasted."

"I personally would like to keep living," Mx. Hyde said. "How about you two?"

"All in favor of living." Medusa extended her hand, and Mx. Hyde and Roxanne pressed their hands on top of hers.

"To living!" Roxanne said, then pulled back her arm. "Which will be easier, I should mention, if we wait until tomorrow night."

"It has been a while." Dr. Hyde glanced up at the sky-light, where the sun was indeed beginning to peep in.

"One more night of slumber party for you, it seems," Roxanne said.

The librarian gestured to her spider friends. "Shall I have them prepare some webs?"

The Monsters Three shared looks among them. "Why not?" Roxanne said, and that day, they slept tangled in sticky webbing.

"I'm starving," Roxanne said the moment she woke.

Mx. Hyde furrowed their eyebrows. "You're up for this, aren't you?" they said. "Three innocents, and we're toast."

Roxanne rubbed her empty belly, which throbbed with lack, as they walked the hallways to the biography room. She had seen a vampire once who had gone too long without food. He was wasted, a sack of skin and bone too weak to move, alive in the dark of his coffin forevermore. He had begged Roxanne to bring him blood, to free him from the constant dying that had become his life, but Roxanne was never keen on the male bloodsuckers, not after she'd experienced their massive egos; they were no match for her own.

"It takes months for vampires to become malnourished," Mx. Hyde said. They gathered their knife and syringes from the shelf upon which they had placed them. "Don't be so dramatic."

Roxanne had no goods to gather. Medusa kept her book clutched to her chest as they made their way out. This time they left through the front door, without saying goodbye to the librarian, and walked in silent excitement through the tunnel that led to town.

At the edge of town, the air was hot, and Mx. Hyde wiped at the sweat accumulating on their forehead. Roxanne blessed her body that it did not sweat. Medusa never blessed her body; it brought her too much pain. She longed to stare and be stared into in return. Her snakes, on the other hand, writhed inside her skull.

The tavern was empty and full of blood.

"I'm the luckiest vampire in the world." Roxanne grabbed a glass from the bar and bent to the floor to scoop blood into it. That was when she heard the groaning. It came from behind the bar. "Hello?" She peered back there. The bartender lay half-bled-out, his body sliced from neck to groin, the skin pulled back and secured open with the help of two needles. His organs were exposed. He looked delicious.

"Help . . . me." He groaned again.

"There is no helping you, friend." Mx. Hyde stepped up next to the man. "I'm surprised you're still alive."

"She fed me something," he said. "Something to keep me from bleeding too fast."

"Snake venom, perhaps," Hyde said. "Or a massive dose of cobalt."

"Does it matter?" Roxanne sipped at her glass of blood. "Is this yours?"

"It's my tavern," he said. "You know that."

"No, is this your blood?" She smacked her lips. "Not the worst I've ever had."

Medusa stood behind Roxanne and delivered a gentle kick to her friend's backside.

"Where did she go?" Roxanne asked.

"You won't believe this," the man said. "It was our barmaid. Our very own barmaid. I bedded her once, you know, and this . . ."

"Yes, we know," Mx. Hyde said. "Now where did she go?"

"To . . . hell," he said, and his eyes clouded over. He coughed, and his organs pushed out from his open belly, and his blood splattered onto Roxanne's face. She pursed her lips and wiped it from her eyes. She licked her fingers.

"He's dead to us." She laughed at herself.

"He's still breathing," Medusa said.

"That he is." Roxanne stood up. "A little blood hit the spot. And no pesky killing of an innocent! I believe we've found a loophole, ladies and gentlepeople."

Roxanne studied the grotesque room. Beside the fireplace, a man had been skinned alive. His flesh lay in a pile beside his leftover muscle, which still bore his shape. At one of the tables in the back, a person had been torn apart and his limbs arranged in the chairs as though they were having drinks, his disembodied hands wrapped around full mugs of ale, his disembodied legs and feet propped with toes stuck into the handle of a giant mug.

"She has an eye for this," Roxanne said, and Mx. Hyde mmm-hmmmed as they retrieved a single piece of hair dangling from one of the beers. "What are you doing? We're not testing her DNA, Hyde."

Hyde slipped the hair inside their pocket. "Why not?"

Roxanne rolled her eyes but continued her exploration of the premises, trying to find out where her lady love had gone off to. She stepped into the kitchen and gasped at the beauty of the scene before her: the barmaid—no, Needleskin, she deserved a monster name if anyone deserved a monster name—had left several steaks of human meat dangling over the sink. Their blood was dripping down into the ceramic. The sink was clogged with gore. Blood boiled in a cast iron cauldron over a fire left burning, and the kitchen smelled of cinnamon and nutmeg. Roxanne felt as though the feast had been constructed for her benefit, but it was impossible, wasn't it, that Needleskin would know who she was?

Roxanne grabbed a sparkling clean wine glass from a cabinet of crystal clearly reserved for special occasions. She filled it with the boiling blood and took a sip. Needleskin had spiced the blood. If not for her benefit, then for whose?

Roxanne emerged from the kitchen, light on her feet, light in her head. She remembered the woman she'd watched with such curiosity and wondered what she looked like now, with so much darkness inside her.

"What's made you so giddy?" Mx. Hyde asked.

Roxanne took another sip of mulled blood. It warmed her belly.

"Where did you get that?" Mx. Hyde said, worry creeping into her voice.

"A gift," Roxanne said. "Needleskin has left for me a gift."

Mx. Hyde frowned. "That's impossible," they said. "How could she possibly know that you were coming for her?"

Medusa worried at her nails. It was a bad habit she took on in times of crisis. Roxanne hated it; she had such beautiful nails when she wasn't picking them bloody. Besides, it made Roxanne hungry to watch the red fill up the crease between skin and nail.

"Why do you both look so disturbed?" Roxanne said.

"It's nothing," Mx. Hyde said. "It's just—pretty woman, courtship. You tend to—"

"I see." Roxanne downed the rest of her warm blood drink. "Once more, you think I can't control myself. You think I fall prey to any gorgeous woman's charm."

Hyde shrugged. "You said it, not me."

"Do we need to rehash this?" Medusa said. "I thought we already recovered from this fight."

"Those other woman I've gone gaga for," Roxanne said. "How many of them are still alive?"

Hyde held out their palms in their typical gesture of peace. "You're right. You get the job done. Eventually."

"Eventually." Roxanne scoffed. "I'm going to take a look at the rest of this place, try to figure out where this so-called trap is taking us next." Roxanne stormed out of the bar and into the attached bedrooms, which the bar owner sometimes rented to out-of-town folks too intoxicated to climb back into their carriages. She found those rooms completely clean, the beds made, extra linens folded at the footboards. The floors had been mopped. The rooms smelled of the fresh lavender flowers Needleskin had placed upon the pillows. "Oh, she is an odd one," Roxanne said to herself.

"I found your lady friend," Mx. Hyde said from the bedroom entryway. They stepped forward and thrust the Living History at Roxanne.

Roxanne opened the book to the latest filled-in page. New words had appeared there. They detailed Needleskin's acceptance into a local brothel. She had pretended to be in need of money and willing to do anything to earn it. She killed her first John and nestled what was left of his body in the wool of her mattress. She was excited by the idea of the other prostitutes finding the mass of bodies she planned to pile up.

"The brothel," Mx. Hyde said. "I know where that is."

"Of course you do," Roxanne said.

Chapter Seven

The Monsters Three walked the cobbled streets arm-in-arm until they came to the red double door that closed the brothel off to the world outside. Mx. Hyde knocked four times. The woman who opened the door had wide hips and a bare belly. She leaned against the doorframe.

"Well, Dr. Hyde," she said. Her voice was gravelly. "It's been a while."

"Been dead," Mx. Hyde said.

"That's a shame," the woman said. "Though, fewer of my girls have gone missing as of late."

"What a coincidence," Mx. Hyde said.

"You can't come in here," the woman said. "I have to take care of my girls."

"Do you know who we are?" Hyde said. The woman scanned each of them up and down. What a sight they must have been: the slender vampire with lips redder than any lipstick could make them; the famished half-man, half-woman Mx. Hyde; and the curly-haired curvy-bodied woman in chaste white who did not seem able to look up from her shoes.

"I don't care." The woman slammed the door in their faces.

"Went well," Roxanne said.

"There's a fire escape." Mx. Hyde gestured behind the building. "Yonder."

"Lovely." Roxanne led the three to the alleyway. Hyde grabbed hold of the fire escape ladder and pulled it down, but Roxanne stuck her hands to the brick and began to climb the smallest holds available. She reached the window and, with a final glance to her slow companions, pushed open the window and climbed inside.

The room was red everywhere but the walls: red silk on the bed, a red rug, and a red scarf draped across the electric lantern on the wall. The room's red light made it darker than most rooms the humans occupied, but Roxanne had no issue seeing in the dark. The room was empty of people. She pressed her ear to the closed door that led into the rest of the brothel and listened for some idea of what was happening out there.

Her ear was accosted by a change in background sound as an anvil clanged. Roxanne pulled back from the door and clutched her hands over her over-sensitive ears. The doorknob turned as a chain rattled. Roxanne backed away and stumbled onto the bed. She flailed to settle herself as the door opened. As a shadow formed in the doorway, Roxanne heard sounds like nothing she had ever heard before. They seemed to be made not by instruments, not by anything she had experienced in her many years in the world. She could not explain it, but they seemed to made by things that humans had made and not by humans at all.

Needleskin dropped the body she had been hoisting over her shoulder. The John landed with a thud on the ground.

"I've been waiting for you," Needleskin said.

She looked like the barmaid in only the most basic of ways. Her hair still curled to her shoulders in a way that signaled that she was, beneath the monstrosity, the woman once known as Deenie. The rest of her was altogether changed. Her features had been rearranged, pulled back in odd angles and pinned with needles. She wore no clothes, and she had stuck herself with needles in a grid from her neck to her calves. Streams of blood had dried on her skin from where she'd pierced herself. She was untouchable, Roxanne realized with a start, and that made Roxanne want to touch her.

"How did you know I was coming for you?" Roxanne said.

"I know about the basest desires," Needleskin said. "I saw you watching me, when I worked in the tavern. I understood what you were then, and now I understand what you want."

"What do I want?" Roxanne felt the blood she had consumed heating again inside her.

"You want so many nasty things, Roxanne." Needleskin stepped forward. "Right now, you want to run your tongue over every sharp point you see. You want to drink the blood of every working girl in this brothel. You want them to moan into your ear as you drain them. You saw what I left for you in the tavern, and you wanted to outdo me even as you wanted to join me."

"I know what you want, too," Roxanne said. "You want pleasure so deep it feels like you're being torn apart."

"We're a happy pair," Needleskin said.

At the open window, Medusa's hand grasped hold of the sill.

"Your friends don't want what you want. That one? I can't even read her." Needleskin pointed a nail-less fingernail at the window. "Your other friend? Oh, that one is driven by curiosity. There's nothing base in that at all."

Roxanne stood from the bed, suddenly sure in her movements, and advanced to the window. She pulled it shut on Medusa's fingers, and Medusa screamed as she let go and fell back with a clang onto the fire escape. Roxanne locked the window latch.

They were monsters, the three of them, and it was time that her friends remembered that. It was time that they remembered that she was the most monstrous of them all.

"That a girl," Needleskin said, moving toward her.

"I aim to please." Roxanne pulled shut the shades and turned to face the woman.

"I like to hear that," she said. She gestured to the groaning man in the doorway. Blood leaked into the carpet around his body. "Do you want a taste?"

"You go ahead." Roxanne passed Needleskin, brushing her shoulder against the stabbing needles as she went. "I'd like to see how you work." Roxanne returned to her seat on the edge of the bed and folded her hands primly in her lap. She ignored the knocking of Mx. Hyde at the window.

"Your friends will find a way inside," Needleskin said.

"It may take a while. Your mistress doesn't much like the doctor."

Needleskin's head whipped to stare Roxanne down, and she traveled in remarkably few steps to reach Roxanne and grip her neck in her hand. "I have no mistress."

"Fine," Roxanne croaked. Needleskin let go. "No need for hysterics."

"You want to see hysterics?" Needleskin grinned, and the needles flexed in her flesh. She stepped to the man, grabbed his arm, and dragged him across the floor. He called out gently, but he was on death's door—Roxanne could smell it. Needleskin rolled the man over, and his dick flopped out of the pants that were wrapped around his ankle. "I admire men their simple desires."

"I do too," Roxanne said, enraptured with Needleskin even more so than she had ever been with the barmaid.

"This one wanted to pillow fight." Needleskin's laugh was like two sticks rubbing together. She knelt beside him as if to pray. With one fingernail, she slit him down his naked belly. "Are you sure you don't want to play?" she asked Roxanne, but Roxanne shook her head, and Needleskin continued. One by one, she removed the organs. At some point, the man died. Needleskin offered each part to Roxanne and waited for Roxanne's gentle refusal before setting them in a circle to her side. The heart she held longer than the rest, and Roxanne's belly growled to see the lovely organ pump its final spurt of blood as Needleskin squeezed it.

"No, thank you," she said, and ached as Needleskin set it to the side with the rest. It felt good to resist when she knew she would eventually give in.

"It's your choice," Needleskin said.

Needleskin finished emptying the man's body cavity. She raised one hand toward the doorway, and a pillow flew from the other room toward her. She ripped it open, pulled out the feathers, and stuffed the man with them. She closed the flaps of his skin and lay her head upon him.

"As soft as the one I used to steal from my older brother," she said.

"Were you always given less than him?" Roxanne asked.

"No," Needleskin said. "But I always wanted more."

Roxanne sunk to her knees. "You said you would give me hysterics. But I saw only meticulousness."

Needleskin picked up her head and grabbed the heart from the floor. "The hysterics are yet to come." She sunk her teeth into one side of the organ. She did not have to tell Roxanne to do the same. Roxanne understood this woman, her every urge. Roxanne bit down, her face inches from Needleskin's, her breath sharing space amongst the blood and muscle. Roxanne did not even much mind that she was, once more, dining on a man, after so many years of avoiding them. She did wonder if she would ever again eat a woman, and she smiled to herself at the thought. They ate until their lips touched, and needles pressed into Roxanne's skin, and the woman, the monster, called Needleskin hiked up Roxanne's red dress and buried her pointed fingernail in Roxanne's body until Roxanne cried out in pain and pleasure both.

They touched one another until they were both covered in blood, until they had both writhed so desperately against the floor that the man's blood and Needleskin's blood and the stolen blood that moved through Roxanne formed an abstraction of red on the wood and the rug. Every kiss delivered to Needleskin required work to find a path through the needles stuck into her skin to the chapped softness of her mouth. She tasted like death and oranges and smelled like wine in the throat after too much drinking.

Roxanne consumed her every inch.

"You're something else," Roxanne said. She had not loved a woman since her first—that friend she had longed for, a lady she had been too late to save with the kiss of forever death. Because after she had made it through that maze all those years ago, after she slaughtered her first family of victims, after she embraced the new bloodthirst in her body, Roxanne returned to the home she had once known. She knocked at the door of that friend: now that she was all-powerful, one with death and fear, she possessed the strength to take her friend into her arms and kiss her like she had never been kissed: upon her neck. Roxanne would make her first vampire. Together, they would rule the world.

Her best friend's father opened the door.

"Roxanne, what are you doing here so late?" He wore all black.

It had been natural, her best friend's death. Or at least that's what they called it, but Roxanne knew now that this was a platitude to ease the grieving. There was no need for true death. Her walking death was as natural as her best friend's body in the ground.

Needleskin and Roxanne stared into one another, the iris, the sclera, the clit of the eye, which Needleskin begged Roxanne to lick. "I want you to gape my maw," Needleskin said, and Roxanne gaped every maw across Needleskin's wounded body. They tore each other apart, the way that lovers do.

"Would you ever let me turn you?" Roxanne asked Needleskin as she lay beside her after. "Your lust for pain. Your lust. Whatever that thing was you did where you summoned the pillow. Plus a vampire's immortality and strength? Can you imagine!"

"I am bound to the plane that made me," Needleskin said, and said no more.

A woman screamed at the door. Roxanne's head jerked. The brothel owner stared at the mess of man the women had made. "Monsters!" she yelled.

"Correct." Roxanne rose to her feet. "You didn't know just by looking at us?" She held the woman in her thrall.

"I don't judge on looks," the brothel mistress tranced.

"I do," Roxanne said. She peered down at Needleskin, who still lay basking in blood. They had done such damage together. Needleskin had done such damage for Roxanne's benefit, to win Roxanne's favor. Needleskin deserved a tribute of equal measure. The barmaid had no mistress. Roxanne would make sure of that. "You look like the tastiest of treats." Roxanne moved to the door, to the woman, and yanked her head to one side. She met eyes with Needleskin and sunk her teeth into the brothel owner's neck. The blood that flowed over her tongue was sweet as a blackberry pie, as rich as a buttery crust, as smooth as expensive satin.

It was not until she let the woman's body drop and felt the clarity of satisfaction move through her that she remembered two things: that she was not supposed to kill innocents, and that her friends were nowhere to be found.

"Where are my friends?" she said mostly to herself, not expecting Needleskin to fake a shy wiggle of her hips, hands clasped chastely in front of her out-and-proud cunt. "Wait, where are they? Do you know?"

"I've been taking care of them," Needleskin said.

Roxanne rushed to the window and yanked up the curtains. She didn't see anyone down in the alley. She rushed from the room, jumping over the wilted bodies, and through the hallway, past bedrooms with closed doors and bedrooms with open doors—the writhing bodies inside didn't seem bothered by the screams that rang out only moments before—and down the staircase, flying so quickly and with so much air beneath her that she almost felt herself morphing into one of her winged forms. But her feet landed against the bottom of the staircase, and she found herself in a room full of pastel couches and pink light. Women sat cross-legged on couches. Others sat with legs spread wide, comfortable in the company of friends. Roxanne did not let herself get distracted. Instead, she threaded her way through the furniture and threw open the door.

Chapter Eight

In the street outside the brothel, Mx. Hyde and Medusa were suspended in midair. Medusa smiled when she saw Roxanne, while Mx. Hyde scowled. Which was fair, considering what Roxanne had been up to. Roxanne wiped a spot of blood from her mouth.

"See? I didn't hurt them." Needleskin gripped Roxanne's shoulder from behind her. Roxanne felt aroused and repulsed by her touch.

"You're doing that?" Roxanne asked. She had thought the thing with the pillow had been a small trick, nothing more, but Needleskin had held these monsters in place, in the air, without even seeming distracted. She wielded more power than Roxanne had previously believed. "Let them go."

"I like having control of them," Needleskin said.

Roxanne turned and wrapped her hands around Needleskin's neck, but the needles kept her from closing in on the skin. Needleskin pushed down on Roxanne's arm, freeing herself.

"Trying to break my concentration?" she said. "I could keep them suspended for the rest of their lives—from a hundred miles away."

Roxanne sunk into herself, shortened her body. She grew fur and claws. She hissed and climbed Needleskin, using the woman's piercings to pull herself up, tugging the holes in the woman's skin as she ascended. Needleskin stumbled backward as Roxanne reached into the spaces unmarred and sunk her claws into the woman. Needleskin tried to throw the cat off, but Roxanne was tangled in the mess of skin and spike.

Roxanne reached Needleskin's face, hooked her claw in a tangle of needles, and pulled as hard as she could.

Roxanne fell to the ground, landing on her feet. She jumped back. Blood arced from Needleskin's now-open wounds as she screamed. Roxanne's body stretched back into its humanesque form, and Mx. Hyde and Medusa fell to the ground amidst Needleskin's broken concentration. There was no reaching beyond unexpected pain; this Roxanne understood as a connoisseur of suffering.

Needleskin quieted and lunged at Roxanne. They fell to the ground. They rolled back and forth in a poor approximation of their prior engagement. Roxanne untangled herself from her lover's body and bolted indoors, past the crowd of onlookers, into the room that had emptied as the prostitutes and their clients fled outside to watch the action.

"We should get paid for this," Roxanne said as Needleskin burst through the door. Roxanne was quick. She would always be quicker than anyone with whom she lay. In the time it took Needleskin to follow, Roxanne had arranged herself on the far side of the room, one elbow crooked against a grand piano, elegant and seductive in her posture. "They all got quite the show out there."

Needleskin did not grin, her mouth slack now that the needles no longer pinned back her lips. "I thought we were something," she said. She gestured at the wall, and it creaked and shuddered as a barrage of nails uncorked themselves from the house's frame, flew through the air, and gathered at Needleskin's feet. The house groaned in its instability. "I thought we could be enough to tear the house down."

Roxanne faked a laugh. "You're just as cheesy as my companions out there."

"They will never accept us," Needleskin said. "That's why I did what I did. That's why I had in store for them— what you could never bear to do."

"I won't let you harm them." Roxanne flew across the room and had her arm around Needleskin's neck before Needleskin could blink, her eyes so newly released from their eternal open. "But I cannot harm you either." She kissed the woman on her smooth cheek. She loved the barriers the needles provided, such a grotesque way to keep people out, admirable as sin, but Roxanne adored the smooth, bloody holes left behind by her attack just the same. "Go. Or it will be three against one, and I will not be on your side."

Needleskin removed herself from Roxanne's grasp as easily as she had removed the nails from the walls. "I could win," she said. "But I don't wish to. It's not competition I'm after. Fighting you would not bring me pleasure." She grabbed Roxanne's face and kissed her hard upon her lips. "Goodbye, Roxanne." And she walked off toward a secret back door of which Roxanne was not yet aware, and as she went, she called down the walls, and they tumbled upon her orders, and covered Roxanne in their debris.

It took Roxanne an hour to dig herself out, and when she emerged into the night, she found her friends also working to uncover her. They embraced.

"Did you kill her?" Dr. Hyde asked as they pulled away. "Can I mark Needleskin off my list?" They raised one eyebrow and smirked.

"I did," Roxanne said. "And there's a woman somewhere in this rubble, for your extraction, Doctor. I know you haven't been able to inject any serum since I brought you back."

Mx. Hyde studied the massive pile of debris. "Where was she?"

"Upstairs," Roxanne said. "You should be able to sniff her out, that snout of yours."

Hyde screwed up their mouth in a half-snarl, but they placed one foot forward into the mess, then the other, and disappeared behind a half-standing wall.

"You killed that woman you sent Hyde after, didn't you?" Medusa said.

"I did." Roxanne shrugged. "It's in my blood. As Hyde always says."

"Why did you make that deal?" Medusa brushed dirt off the ass of her dress. She straightened the garment to ensure that it fell properly across her body. "We all understand you, you know. That deal? He made that because he understands you too."

Roxanne huffed. "I killed Needleskin, didn't I?"

"Didn't you?" Medusa said.

Mx. Hyde returned from their extraction; it had always been a quick process.

"Feeling better?" Medusa said.

Hyde reached into their pocket and pulled out a pair of syringes, the only two that had remained intact throughout their death and revival.

"Don't you need to take it?" Roxanne said.

"I took a dose," Hyde said. "This one is for later."

"Good," Roxanne said. "Wouldn't want Mister Jackoff to take over." Roxanne pulled Hyde in and kissed their cheek. "Ol Chap ruins everything."

"Do I speak ill of your old form?" Mx. Hyde said. "Then don't speak ill of mine."

"Fine, fine," Roxanne said. She looped her arms around both her friends. "Off to our next fight?"

Mx. Hyde gestured between two buildings to the east, where the sun was starting to peak across the horizon. Roxanne heaved a sigh, but Mx. Hyde led her forward, toward an old dress shop across the street. Hyde jimmied the lock with a hairpin until the door popped open.

"And the owners?" Medusa asked as they swept inside.

"I stepped over her body," Mx. Hyde said, "in the rubble."

They shut the door, and the Monsters Three formed their makeshift lair in the back room with three nests of fine silk garments, and an undressed mannequin bust for Roxanne's pillow.

Chapter Nine

Night crept forth on jagged talons. Or maybe it was just the constant tap of mosquitos hitting the front window at the full force of their flight. Roxanne woke refreshed, and Medusa always slept like stone, but Mx. Hyde disentangled from their makeshift bed with bags under their eyes.

"What are those damn bugs up to?" they asked, peering out the front window.

"Mosquitos and I understand one another," Roxanne said. "Leave them alone."

"I didn't sleep a wink," Mx. Hyde said. They pressed their hand against the glass and watched as the mosquitos formed the shape of their palm on the other side. Medusa examined the window. "Do you get the feeling that—" Hyde started.

"They're trying to tell us something?" Medusa asked.

"Precisely." Dr. Hyde removed their hand from the glass, and the mosquitos dispersed, then formed once more a cloud and banged against the glass.

"I'm telling you, they're here for me." Roxanne slipped on her dress and kicked her own nest of garments aside. "Bloodsucker love." But in her belly, she feared that they were here for more than kinship. After all, mosquitos were adorned with needles too.

"No, wait." Dr. Hyde pulled open the bag they'd stowed on the floor the night previous. They pulled out the book the librarian gave them and opened it to a random page. "I thought so! It says here that Zeeka was doing experiments on mosquitos. I bet they're here to lead us to her!"

"And who sent them, exactly?" Roxanne asked.

"Inconclusive," Dr. Hyde said. "Only one way to find out."

Roxanne groaned, but Medusa placed her hand on Dr. Hyde's shoulder. "We're going with you," she said.

"Of course, yes," Roxanne said, but her head throbbed with the possibility that they may walk right into a trap set for them by Needleskin. "We are here to help."

They gathered their belongings—Hyde their bag, Roxanne her dirty undergarments, and Medusa the beloved book that had not left the hem of her own undergarments since the librarian gave it to her—and opened the front door.

The mosquitos did not swarm toward them. Instead, they formed a line before the Monsters Three that led back in the direction of the tavern and the woods and the Great Library of Evil's hidden location. Every step they took on the cobblestone made Roxanne's body tremble. She longed to once more touch the woman called Needleskin—and she wished to never see her again in her long, forever-life.

The monsters walked. Roxanne with her smooth gait that looked, to the common eye, as though she floated. Mx. Hyde strode confidently, always with one hand buried in their pocket, likely fingering some scientific object or the tip of their blade. Medusa watched the sky, her pupils full of moon. The streets were empty, the townspeople finally frightened of the bad things that threatened their lives after the destruction of their brothel and the gruesome scene at their tavern. Roxanne took in the scent of their fear as they passed their half-open windows. She enjoyed it like she used to enjoy the smell of the streets after the rain, when all the shit and piss had washed away and the wet stone was cool beneath her feet.

The monsters arrived at the tunnel that had taken them from the library to town. The mosquitos grew more agitated, but they did not dive down into the tunnel's wet embrace. Instead, they swarmed farther into the woods.

"Are we really about to walk right into some monster's trap?" Roxanne swatted at the mosquitos in front of her face. Screw pacts, among bloodsuckers and others.

Mx. Hyde slapped her on the back. "You love a good trap," they said, then paused. "Are you feeling okay? You look feverish." They pressed their hand against Roxanne's forehead.

Medusa's attention was caught, and she was once more part of the world. "Is she ill? Do we need to rest?"

Roxanne swatted them away like they were mosquitos. But even though she owned no blood of her own inside her body, she warmed at the concern of her friends. The effect had always confused her. "Let's go."

Each step sent up the smell of wet, molding leaves. Dark shadows passed over their faces. In the distance, a rumbling organ played in time with the groaning of tree limbs. The Monsters Three followed the mosquitos to a half-rotted tree in the woods. They approached a dark cloud of mosquitos, and the background organ faded into a trio of gentle woodwinds. Roxanne parted the cloud with both hands. The mosquitos danced through her open fingers. She closed her mouth and eyes and reached out until she felt something: a massive tree trunk. She could not see it for the mosquitos clouding her vision, but she could feel the soft rot of wood underneath her fingers. She shivered to remember the soft mess of Needleskin's lips. She pulled at a strip of bark, and it fell away. She kept pulling. Beside her, she heard her friends do the same, until Medusa's small shriek rang out. Roxanne stepped around the tree, feeling for Medusa, fearing for the worst—that Needleskin had indeed lured them here, had shoved some blade into Medusa's flesh—but instead, her hand pressed suddenly against nothing, and she fell forward, losing her footing as the deep well swallowed her.

Roxanne landed on her ass. She opened her eyes. The mosquitos had gone. Beside her sat Medusa. Around them, copper walls. Below them, a cold copper floor. Woodwinds gave way to a swell of brass, and Roxanne understood that they had stumbled upon something altogether different from Needleskin's hedonism, which was composed of sounds divorced from harmony. Before them loomed a metal door, round with a round metal handle like a wheel with no spokes. Above them, Hyde let out one deep yelp then slid into them from behind.

Roxanne stood and peered up the tunnel down which they had all fallen. It was dirt until about halfway, when it became metal slippery enough to deliver three monsters to this secret entrance.

"This must be the place." Hyde stood and dusted themself off. They went to the door and ran their hand along it. "Sterile."

Roxanne had no quip, overcome with relief that her friends' doom did not await them.

Mx. Hyde grabbed hold of the metal wheel and turned until the door gave, then pulled. The door swung open. The air that surged from inside the laboratory was odorless, the light as bright and unforgiving as Roxanne remembered summer light could be. They stepped inside, one after the other, and Roxanne examined her ashy skin beneath the buzzing lights. She looked deader than she'd ever looked. She looked marvelous. The strange lights sounded like mosquitos.

"Is my skin so grey?" Medusa said, examining her own arm.

"You're lovely." Roxanne took her hand. She wanted to squeeze both their hands, to take them into her arms and apologize for the mess of her love and for the half-desire she had for Needleskin to tear them all apart, but Dr. Hyde had already explored so far into the laboratory that there was no reaching out for them.

When Medusa and Roxanne stepped free from the blank copper hall that led into the lab, they found a room with two copper beehive machines on either end. Coils topped the machines, and experiments bubbled in every corner. Two doors stood closed on the other side of the room. Mx. Hyde was examining the beehives. Roxanne stood beside them. The beehives seemed to be little rooms of some kind, with doors and a small glass window. Roxanne tried to look inside, but it was too dark to see. The hives were big enough for one, perhaps two people to sit comfortably, and no more.

"What are they?" Roxanne asked.

"I wonder," Mx. Hyde said. They moved on to the experiments, and Roxanne and Medusa stood aside. "The book said that Zeeka studied transmogrification."

"Which is . . ." Roxanne said.

"To transmogrify is to change form," Dr. Hyde said, sniffing a test tube.

"Like what you do?" Roxanne said. "With your serum?"

"What I did," Dr. Hyde said. "I wouldn't call myself active in the field."

"Oh, doc, you still take the serum. To be half-and-half. To not go back to old boy Jekyll or be all Ms. Hyde. That sounds active to me," Medusa said in her most uplifting voice. It was sweet the way she tried to reassure them of their worth to the world, even as she denied her own. "You're still a scientist."

"My lab is abandoned," Dr. Hyde said. They shoved their hands in their pockets, then pulled put the dead mosquito. "I'd forgotten I saved this."

Medusa laughed. "And you say you're not a scientist?"

"What's that you've got there?" a voice said, and the Monsters Three glanced about. "One of mine?"

Roxanne looked up. On the ceiling, the mosquito woman hung from one of the long humming lights. She buzzed down, graceful for a pest, and landed on human feet attached to spindly insectile legs. She had two abdomens, both bare: the mosquito segments poked out behind her while her human abdomen revealed the ribs beneath. Two insectile arms ended in human hands, and atop her head, where hair should be, were two bug eyes like buns, with a proboscis in the middle of her forehead. Two antennae twitched beside her ears. She looked like she had not eaten in ages.

Chapter Ten

"And who are you?" she asked, scanning them each. From behind her shuffled a lobotomized woman, a zombie of a creature, holding a scalpel, ready to defend.

"Don't you know?" Dr. Hyde said. "Your mosquitos led us here."

Zeeka laughed. "They aren't very bright." She moved toward them and circled the Monsters Three. "They are trained to bring me blood. And this one." She gestured to her assistant. "Is trained to bring me other things I require from the outside world. But you—" Her proboscis extended and pricked Roxanne's shoulder. "You're a bloodsucker, and you—" She gestured at Medusa. "Your blood is too old. And you—" She paused before Dr. Hyde. "Well, you'll do." Her assistant lurched forward, and Dr. Hyde jumped back. Zeeka tilted her head, and it seemed as though her four eyes were cataloguing every split detail of Dr. Hyde's face, their body, their clothes. "Grovel, stop. Come here, Grovel." The assistant lowered her weapon and swayed from side to side, then moved back to stand beside her master. "I'm only kidding, of course. You are my guests." She gestured at Dr. Hyde. "I want to know all about you, dear. Won't you sit and talk to me, all three of you?"

Roxanne scanned the lab again; there was no seating present.

"Follow me," Zeeka said, and she lifted slightly off the ground and buzzed through the lab, to the right back door, which she opened. They followed her through. The room was full of copper morgue tables, a nostalgic sight; Roxanne missed raiding morgues, finding the freshest bodies and availing them of their blood before the undertakers wasted such lovely treats.

"Please, sit, sit." Zeeka gestured at the tables. She landed on one and dangled her legs over the side. "Dr. Hyde, here," and she patted the space beside her. Her assistant did not follow them inside.

Dr. Hyde shrugged and hoisted themself onto the table. "How did you afford this lab?"

"I sell things. Solutions and such. In the blackest markets."

"Around here?" Roxanne said. She had not discovered the wicked underbelly of this town; perhaps it was not as boring as she thought it was.

"There's a lot of people who want to be other than they are," Zeeka said.

"Your solutions grant the user . . . transmogrification?" Dr. Hyde reached into their pocket, and a dreamy look came over their face. "Mosquitos only? Or other insects?"

"Insects. Arachnids." Zeeka's face also transformed, but into something sad and wanting. "It's only mammals that I haven't cracked."

As Dr. Hyde and Zeeka spoke, Medusa and Roxanne settled onto their own tables. Roxanne watched the scene unfold before them and understood it all: this would be Dr. Hyde's temptation, and if they failed like Roxanne had failed, then there was small chance of defeating the Guardian.

"We must compare notes, you and me," Zeeka said, and she placed her hand upon Mx. Hyde's leg and squeezed. Roxanne and Medusa shared a glance. "Tell me everything there is to know about you."

Roxanne knew the story of Mx. Hyde's transformation, of their past names, of their past faces, but she listened as her friend told the mosquito woman the story of their life.

Dr. Hyde or Mx. Hyde: Hyde minded neither moniker, but once they went by another name, two names in fact, that no longer fit with the makeup of their DNA. Dr. Hyde's old name belonged to a man with a face that brought barmaids to their knees. A scientist, Dr. Hyde was a sought-after gentleman, but Dr. Hyde cared not for romance. Dr. Hyde longed for one thing alone: panacea. For Dr. Hyde felt ill most days of their life, and no doctor seemed capable of diagnosing them.

Dr. Hyde spent every day in their little apartment with their back-bedroom laboratory. The first serum they extracted from the pineal gland of a cadaver—a nameless beggar woman—and it tasted like green olives and shone as brightly as silver in a candle's light. They swallowed it like it was the only sustenance they had ever tasted.

The other half that emerged was nothing like the barmaids with which they sometimes consorted. No, Dr. Hyde's other half was a woman half-feral in her gaze, more like Roxanne than Medusa, and the woman hungered: for meat, of all varieties. In this form, Dr. Hyde consumed turkey legs in the local tavern and let the flesh fall down their face. They dragged a woman into a back room and had them against whatever surfaces presented themselves. They wanted, and the thing they wanted most came to be control—of the body, of the ability to exist, but they were a visitor in the world. It was the other half, the scientist, who controlled the skin in which they dwelled.

Their first night, when Dr. Hyde felt the woman fading away, they searched the house for more serum but found nothing. Dr. Hyde had made enough for one night only—and to create more would require the harvesting of more bodies.

In the morning, Dr. Hyde woke a man, a scientist, and in their belly, they ached for something they had never had. They remembered pieces of that other life. Had they felt free from affliction? They remembered only ecstasy.

They paid the local morgue for another cadaver. They extracted the necessary hormones. They concocted another serum. Then another. And another, until the morgue ran out of bodies, and Dr. Hyde ran out of serum, and the man, the scientist, moped in their apartment while the woman, the adventurer, raged within his skin.

Until she broke as free as she could. She spoke to him as a burning in his organs, a headache that screamed until he cradled his skull in his hands and wailed. Until he lost his thoughts, and hers rushed in to replace them: Find. Another. Woman.

"I can't," he said aloud. "There's been no more deaths."

Make death.

They argued for hours, until they wore themselves down. Then they gathered the blade they carried through the dark and dangerous streets and swept across the cobblestone walkways. They made their way through alleyways. They wore a handsome face, and it was not long before a woman of the night approached them.

She smelled like cinnamon bread, and half of Dr. Hyde resisted the will to see her blood, to examine the way it would spill into the walkway's cracks. Half of Dr. Hyde tried to flee, but the woman in the alleyway was quick, and she grabbed Hyde's hand and forced his fingers between her legs.

"Not every day I meet a good-looking fella like you," she said to them. "A handsome man such as yourself? Well, I imagine I'd let you do things that other men beg me to let them do."

When Hyde pulled their hand away, it reeked of yeast and lust. Part of Hyde wrinkled their nose at the smell, and the other half pulled the woman in for a deep kiss on her lips. They pulled away, and half of them yanked the blade from its hiding place and shoved it deep into the woman's heart. They let her drop to the ground.

Her blood, as it wept from her wound, and trickled down her neck, and soaked through her ruffled collar, and flowed to the ground, looked like a red network of veins through stone flesh.

Hyde was both parts of themselves as they plunged their needle through her forehead and extracted the necessary hormone.

It went on like that for a time, but Hyde transformed into their feminine self to perform the murders. The Ms. was strong, preternaturally so, and to contain illicit behavior to her face made it easier to hide from the newspapers that decried the appearance of a murderous prostitute who preyed on her peers. She was suspected of thinning the competition, and some reporters wondered if she would run her way through the local brothel until she revealed herself to the public by being the only woman left to take the blame. Hyde understood that they would need to leave before that happened, but they put it off, unwilling to abandon the lab that they spent so many years building. The lab that had brought them their greatest breakthrough.

Soon it was not enough for Hyde's feminine side to claim the night and their masculine side to take the day. She wanted out at all hours, and he wanted time into the evening to burn over his experiments. They warred, made themselves sick with inner turmoil that manifested in a pallor that worried the doctor's associates and a frenzied countenance that threatened to tip off passersby to their monstrous nature. They could not go on, and they did not want to leave—and they had no choice but to attempt sabotage upon their own self. The doctor gulped the kerosene from his lantern as he put it out for the night, and the other half came into their body vomiting green bile, changing from man to woman, from woman to man. The woman tried to sabotage the doctor's reputation, claiming affronts to her profession until the police knocked on his door and demanded to inspect the place. The police found nothing, for they had used all the serum they'd saved up, but it became clear as the policeman left but lingered in their carriage outside that this could not go on.

It was the next night, as they plunged their needle into their latest hooker's forehead, as they stepped away from the lifeless body and stepped into a pool of blood, as they looked down to inspect their shoe, and saw their reflection in the puddle, their two faces half-to-half, their two bodies, outfits, requisite parts split down the center, that they realized to what conclusion they'd been forced to come: and Mx. Hyde was born.

"Your story," Zeeka said, hopping down from the operating table, "is fascinating. You did not even mean to create this potion—this miracle of transmogrification!—and yet, here you are!" Zeeka paced. "It is funny, is it not, that so many discoveries are accidental." She looked up, and a glint passed in her eyes. "It is unfair, in a way."

"Unfair?" Hyde asked.

"That some people spend their lives searching, only for others to stumble on the answer." For a moment, Zeeka frowned, and her antennae bent in half like furrowed brows. But then they stood once more upright. "Life, it seems, cannot ever fully be controlled."

"I tend to disagree," Hyde said. "I have controlled life. I have held a woman dying from my blade in my arms. I have returned to life—"

Roxanne cleared her throat to catch Dr. Hyde's attention. After all, they were there because of Hyde's resurrection, to settle the Guardian's score, to force Zeeka into the grave. Weren't they?

Dr. Hyde glanced back at Roxanne and narrowed their eyes.

"This is fascinating." Zeeka buzzed with excitement. "But your friends must be bored to tears!"

"Yes," Dr. Hyde said. "Perhaps they would prefer to take a walk."

Roxanne stood and straightened out her dress, growing more uneasy by the moment. "I understand a dismissal when I hear one." She narrowed her eyes back at Mx. Hyde, then held out her palm to help Medusa from the table. "Shall we?"

Roxanne and Medusa left the room arm in arm, Roxanne moving as though she were leaving a ball—perhaps that very same ball that had been her last as a human woman, perhaps some blood ball she might arrange in the future. She smiled at the thought, but the coldness of the lab through which they walked brought her back to the situation at hand. The mosquito woman's assistant fussed at an experiment and did not even seem to notice them leaving. Were these creatures so dumb as to not see them as threats? No wonder, with Dr. Hyde oohing over Zeeka's facilities like a schoolchild. Roxanne had no right to pressure Dr. Hyde to hurry, no right to pressure Dr. Hyde to succeed when she herself had not, but she wanted nothing more in that moment than to rush back into the room where the two drips shared science tips and take out Zeeka with one swift rip of the throat. She would give her friend one night—and no more. Then they would tackle the monster meant for Medusa. Then, they would find Needleskin, and they would take her down. Or Roxanne would take her down. Or Roxanne would go down. Or Roxanne would—

"That rare expression, Roxanne's thinking face," Medusa said, breaking the reverie.

"Excuse me?" Roxanne said. She stopped and examined their surroundings; somehow, they'd wound up outside, on a hill overlooking town, their legs swarmed with mosquitos in the tall grass. "How did we get here?"

"Secret door," Medusa said. "Were you not listening to Zeeka at all?"

"Partially," Roxanne said.

Medusa threw her arms out as though crucified, then fell back into the grass, disappearing from Roxanne's view. Roxanne crouched to find Medusa resting in the dirt. Roxanne scowled as she patted down some grass and settled uncomfortably beside her.

"What are you thinking about?" Medusa said.

"I think all the time, you know," Roxanne said. The grass made her itch, but she didn't dare scratch her flawless skin. Someone might see. Someone might wish they had scratched it for her.

Medusa giggled. "I'm only teasing."

"Well, I don't like it," Roxanne said, surprised at herself as soon as the words left her mouth.

"You tease all the time," Medusa said, her voice edged with rare irritation. "You two never let me tease."

Roxanne reached out and poked at a mushroom. It bounced under her finger. She pulled her hand back and licked the poison. It tingled on her tongue.

"What's bothering you?" Medusa kicked her shoes into the hidden distance and stretched out her toes. She wiggled them, then sat up. "Oh! Look at that!"

Roxanne thought at first that she was seeing the rotting toes of a dead body. A gift? But once her eyes focused on the toenail mushrooms, she growled.

"Fascinating," she said.

"Seriously, what is bothering you?" Medusa asked.

Roxanne ached between her legs. She ached in her chest where her heart would beat if she had a beating heart. She'd expected the worst from Needleskin. She'd expected something, at least—but Needleskin seemed to have vanished and forgotten all about Roxanne.

"They're awful cozy in there," Roxanne said.

"Hyde and Zeeka?"

Roxanne gave Medusa a withering look.

"You know the doctor would never let an opportunity slip to pick the brain of a fellow scientist. What of it?"

"Mx. sure doesn't seem to have murder on the brain," Roxanne said. "Which, you know, is not at all like them."

"You have to trust them," Medusa said. "Hyde will do the right thing. Like you did, with Needleskin."

Roxanne bit the inside of her lip until it hurt. She needed to feed, but she couldn't feed, not on anyone but the monsters they were supposed to kill. Or those monsters' victims, should they be so lucky as to stumble across some.

"I'm hungry," Roxanne said.

"We'll all have to be hungry for some time," Medusa said. "I feel bad for Hyde, I really do. They must be terrified, not being able to extract—what if they turn back? You and me, we'll survive. Will Hyde?"

"All the more reason to hurry this along." Roxanne started to stand. She understood the issues they faced from hunger: Medusa would turn quiet and slow until she crafted her next stone statue and Mx. Hyde would return to their status quo—revert back to their original body, their original mind, and neither Medusa nor Roxanne wished to meet them that way. Roxanne, on the other hand, would turn feral with hunger. She grinned. That might not be the worst thing, if Needleskin did come to visit. Let her animal brain make the decisions for her. Give in.

Roxanne stood. Right now, nature was too loud and too hot and too coarse, the grass poking even through her red dress, now stained with the stuff. She smoothed the dirty silk and dug the tip of her heel into Medusa's belly.

Medusa cried out, but there was laughter in her voice.

"You asleep?" Roxanne said.

"Let me enjoy the air," Medusa said. "It's awful in there."

"I'm not going back without you." Roxanne ventured farther out. She could use a spot of alone time. "Don't abandon me either."

Roxanne waded through the tall grass until she could no longer tell where Medusa had disturbed it, could no longer tell where Medusa hid like a snake. Her friend was nothing like a snake, except when she was, when she let lust take over and tricked some poor fool into wanting to fall prey to a young maiden's eyes. Medusa claimed innocence. She claimed to be different than her companions in intent, at least, if not in execution. Roxanne had never bought it.

Roxanne chased the waxing crescent moon. It came never closer, and she ran toward it, navigating the grass in her long dress as best as she was able. Finally, she kicked off her shoes and let the dirt cool her feet. Something stabbed her.

She'd stepped on something sharp. She yelped and fell backward into the grass. She held up her foot and inspected: a needle protruded from the skin. She yanked it out, her stomach rolling. She pushed herself back to standing and searched the landscape, but she saw nothing. No one.

Roxanne rolled the needle across her tongue and tasted the dirt, her minimal blood—composed of so many human bloods—and the faintest hint of Needleskin.

Chapter Eleven

Back inside, Zeeka demonstrated another of her inventions. First, she rolled the examination tables to the sides of the room. Then she pressed a button on the wall that activated a series of levers. The levers lowered several copper pods from an opening in the ceiling. The pods hissed then popped open. Inside, they were filled with white foam. Roxanne pressed her palm into the material. It left behind an indentation.

"What are these?" she said.

"Our beds for the evening," Zeeka said. "You are staying the night, aren't you? I'm afraid there's nowhere you could reach before sunup."

Zeeka spoke the truth. Plus, the cushion beneath Roxanne's palm was as soft a coffin as she had experienced. She shrugged off her red dress, letting it soothe to the floor in a puddle. Like blood. Zeeka looked away, though her friends did not. Roxanne climbed into the coffin. "Modest little monster, aren't you?" she said to Zeeka, then shut the top over herself and dozed.

The theremin startled her awake. He hovered in the coffin with her, pressed against her from above.

"A little small for the both of us," the guardian said, then drove his claws into her shoulder. She screamed and pushed the coffin open, and he jumped back into the lifeless room. She pressed her hand against the wound he had inflicted; it was smaller than it should have been. He held up his hand, and instead of bone claws, he had shoved five needles between his knuckles.

"This is what you like, isn't it, vampire heathen?" he said and laughed. "You failed to kill her."

"You better be quiet or you'll wake them," she said. "Can you handle four against one?"

He rushed at her in a blur of smoke that formed a skull, then cackled as he passed through her to the other side of the room. "Wake them? We're all asleep." He motioned into the dark distance. "Except her."

Roxanne scanned the room and saw: Zeeka had pried open the casket containing the sleeping form of Dr. Hyde. The proboscis on her forehead extended down and pierced Hyde's skin.

"And yet you sleep and fail to keep your friends safe." He opened wide his terrible mouth and picked at his teeth with his needle nails. "How much do you really love them? That you can't even put your own desires before theirs?"

Roxanne burst toward Zeeka. She grabbed at her throat, but her hands passed right through.

"I wouldn't have dared wake you," he said. "Bad luck to wake a sleeping vampire."

"Wake me up!" she yelled. "Now!"

"I think you misunderstand who calls the shots." The guardian stepped back three careful steps, until he disappeared into the wall, the only sign of him ever being there the stinging holes in Roxanne's skin that were already closing. "Wake yourself."

Roxanne screamed as her eyes flew open. She was only recently accustomed to waking before the sun went down, and it pained her to rouse from the half-death of a sleeping creature of the night. She pushed open her pod and scurried from it, the same as in her dream, only this time she wasn't weighed down by the specter of death.

Zeeka stood with her long arms crossed awkwardly; they looked like two pieces of straw tangled together. Her proboscis had retracted once more.

"Stay away from them!" Roxanne cried out.

"From who?" Zeeka said. Her buggy eyes seemed smaller, her legs thicker. "Were you having a little nightmare?"

Roxanne rushed forward in a blur of bloodless body, a pale streak on the air. Zeeka lifted up and buzzed back, away from Roxanne, but it was not toward Zeeka that Roxanne rushed. She grasped hold of Mx. Hyde's pod and pulled the lid open with all the force she stored inside. It ripped off its hinges and crashed to the floor. Dr. Hyde sat up, knife at the ready. Roxanne dodged the blade.

"You frightened me," Dr. Hyde said.

"You're okay?" Roxanne said. "Zeeka was draining you in your sleep."

Dr. Hyde furrowed their brow. They massaged the skin of their neck. "Zeeka? I thought it was a dream."

"The only dream was that you might make a friend here instead of doing what we came to do," Roxanne said.

Dr. Hyde scoffed. "Excuse me? And you weren't canoodling with that kinky prostitute for a full hour before you finally decided to off her?"

"Off her?" Zeeka said, her hand searching the wall behind her. Roxanne realized that it was full of hidden slots where Zeeka had clearly hidden implements of her science—or her evil. "What you came here to do?"

"I wasn't making friends," Dr. Hyde said. "I was just—learning. Did you bring me back from the dead just to scold me when I do what I've always loved to do? These experiments—this lab—it's remarkable!"

Zeeka looked down at the floor. "Thank you," she said, an actor after all. "You're remarkable too."

Dr. Hyde shook their head. "Oh sure," they said. "You were draining me! You'd prefer me as a specimen on your table."

"And wouldn't you prefer me that way?" Zeeka advanced. "It doesn't have to be like this, though. We can make a truce. We can work together."

"You were killing me in my sleep!" Dr. Hyde laughed, and Roxanne felt proud of her friend. "Like I could trust you!"

"And her? You can trust her?" Zeeka said.

"Not to kill me, yes. Absolutely. Roxanne brought me back to life!" Dr. Hyde said.

"I wasn't killing you. I was taking a sample. You understand. Knowledge is worth that, isn't it? Leave your whining friends. Join me. We'll take them out together."

Zeeka had something behind her back, hidden in her strange hands. To trust a monster, even her own friend, was a terrible mistake to make. Roxanne kept a keen eye on Zeeka, equally aware that Medusa dozed in another copper pod Zeeka had provided. Roxanne hoped that Medusa was still alive. A creature as primordial as her deserved to watch that final burning of the world. Roxanne aimed to be there for it as well.

"Well, Dr. Hyde? You were friendly with mosquito ma'am. Was it enough to turn you against us?"

Dr. Hyde scanned Roxanne from naked torso to bare feet. They grinned with half their mouth, that most mischievous side, and turned to face Roxanne, allying herself with Zeeka in position.

"You can't be the only one with secrets," Dr. Hyde said.

There it was: inside of Hyde, there must exist, as there existed in Roxanne, some ulterior motive to the friendship they shared. Roxanne had not quite suspected it, but perhaps she had known it as intrinsically as she had known, upon awakening from her human death, how to hunt for blood—perhaps all monsters understood, deep inside, how to take for themselves and leave destruction behind.

Zeeka revealed her weapon: a syringe filled with clear liquid.

Roxanne cocked her head. "Really? Are you sure your medicine works on vampires? We live by different rules, you know."

Zeeka tapped at the syringe like a demented nurse and squirted a thin stream into the air. "I know all about creatures of transformation." Zeeka waved the syringe about. "This is holy water."

Roxanne's heart jumped, then stopped once more; it was a strange sensation, and a strange idea that fear of death might bring her ever slightly closer to humanity. She pressed her hand to her chest. She had seen vampires who had been attacked by holy water, the way their skin was forever marred. Her immortal body was perfect. She did not want to see it turned ugly. Then there was that other fact: she had never seen a vampire injected with the stuff before. It would do to her insides what it did to their outsides. She might walk the world forever rotten—or she might burn up completely.

"Aren't you curious to see what happens?" Zeeka asked Dr. Hyde, never taking her eyes off Roxanne. She stepped forward. Roxanne wanted to run, but she did not want to appear weak. That ailing creature on the other side of the wall might restrain her. She might not get past the doors. Roxanne tried to calculate the best strategy, but quick thinking had never been her strong suit. She was one who moved without thought, an impulsive soul—if she even had one. It was Mx. Hyde, the calculating doctor, who made the plans. It was why they worked so well together: the brawn, the brain, and then Medusa's heart near to bursting.

Roxanne would have to kill the monster herself. And if Dr. Hyde betrayed her—well, then she'd murder two birds with the same stone. She hissed and readied herself to lunge.

"This is what you want," she said to Dr. Hyde. "So be it."

Chapter Twelve

Dr. Hyde did not move or even seem to breathe. Then, in what appeared like one single movement, they reached into their pocket, removed their own syringe full of green liquid, and plunged it into Zeeka's back.

Zeeka fell forward. "What—?" she said, then dropped to her knees. "What have you done?"

As Roxanne watched, Zeeka's skin rippled across her body, and her proboscis extended, then split down its center. She screamed as her insect skin smoothed into human skin, then split along her arms, one half falling away, shedding upon the floor. Beneath was a mess of raw red sores.

Dr. Hyde dropped their syringe and pulled out their knife. They knelt beside Zeeka, pulled back her head, and in one fell swoop severed it from her body. It plunked on the floor. The body withered. Blood leaked in a halo around her.

Medusa's pod opened. She sat up, rubbing sleep from her eyes. Then she saw the scene before her. "What's going on?"

"There are some things more important than knowledge," Dr. Hyde said.

Medusa padded across the floor. "Two down," she said as she stopped to run her fingers across Zeeka's strange, mottled skin. "What happened?"

"I gave her my serum," Dr. Hyde said. "Her body didn't know what to do with it. It's been through so much change. Her hormones weren't human anymore, not truly, and when I introduced my serum, she didn't know what to do with the influx. Male or female—bug or human? In the end, she was all of those things."

Dr. Hyde reached into their pocket and took out a notepad. They scribbled a few notes. "It's interesting."

"Sure," Roxanne said, her fear transformed to guilt. Unlike Hyde, she had not been able to overcome her desires. She was unable to perform selflessness.

Hyde slipped their notebook back into their pocket. They snapped a proboscis from Zeeka's head.

"You've never been one for trophies," Roxanne said.

"This is a scientific tool," Dr. Hyde said. They offered their arms to Roxanne and Medusa. "Shall we?"

As Medusa latched onto Dr. Hyde's left side, she frowned. "Do you have more serum?"

"I do not," Dr. Hyde said.

Roxanne reluctantly attached herself to the doctor's right side. "How long until we look forward to your unfortunate half?"

"I resent that," Mx. Hyde said with only half their face. Then they shrugged. "I haven't been using the serum for a while."

Roxanne let go of their arm. "What do you mean?"

"I mean I don't need it any longer," they said. "I can stay this way without it. I have stayed this way without it since you brought me back."

"You lied to us," Roxanne said, but Medusa's voice overrode hers.

"Congratulations!" Medusa cried. "That's huge. That's what you've always wanted, isn't it?"

Dr. Hyde grinned. "Not always. Once upon a time, I was at war with myself. But yes. This is the outcome I've wished for over the last decade."

Roxanne's stomach growled. Maybe it was the lack of blood filling her up and maybe it was that oldest friend, guilt, or maybe it was that constant companion, dissatisfaction. Roxanne stood with her two friends in that unfeeling lab and understood, finally and totally, that she was altogether different from the fiends to whom she'd hitched her carriage. That they were different—and she was a monster—and what was a monster to do with friends, anyway? She was hungry for sustenance, for true terror, for friendship and for a life that did not involve the feelings of other people. Vampires were indeed a confliction: alive and dead, terrible and beautiful. The thoughts made her wilt, like a corpse might wilt.

"Are you quite all right?" Medusa asked, placing a hand on Roxanne's bare back.

Roxanne shrunk away. She gathered her now-dusty garments and pulled the dress onto her body. Then she spoke. "I'm fine."

"On to the next?" Dr. Hyde said. They waved their new weapon about.

"On to the next," Roxanne said.

They walked together to the door, Dr. Hyde in the lead, Medusa in the middle, and Roxanne at the end of their line. They made their way through the door and into the laboratory. Dr. Hyde and Medusa were content to ignore Zeeka's assistant humming to herself in the corner, but to Roxanne it sounded like a hundred mosquitos. It reminded her of the time she had spent traversing the tunnels alone, before she'd brought back her friends, and it reminded her of the trip to this place, where she had made so many fresh realizations. It reminded her of sitting outside with Medusa and walking and stepping on the needle she had hidden away inside the first layer of the skin of her arm. Mosquitos were bloodsuckers, but they were not like her. No one could ever be like her. She was the vampire harpy, and she knew no analog in nature.

Her friends were three steps ahead of her when she turned, sudden as an unsuspecting gale, and rushed toward the assistant. In one fell swoop, she wrestled the creature to the ground and sunk her teeth deep into her neck, draining her for all she was worth, which, when she pulled back, she realized was very little indeed.

The assistant gasped one final breath. Then what little light had been there fled her eyes. Roxanne wiped at her mouth. The assistant's blood tasted like strange medicine and dried flowers. She'd not been human in the truest sense, and the weight of her blood in Roxanne's belly was heavy. She grimaced and gagged, then recovered as best as she was able.

"This thing is an experiment all its own," she said.

Medusa did as she did best. She knelt to the dead creature and looked into its eyes, but it was too late to save it from pain. When she rose, her pupils reflected a fire that was not in the room.

"You've put us at risk," she said. "Again." She clenched her fist.

"It's fine." Roxanne gripped at Medusa's shoulder. "Everything is fine, my lady. We'll go get yours. We'll beat back the guardian."

Medusa flamed. Her curls moved as the snakes writhed inside, loosening from their tight structure, and Roxanne saw the vague shape of their tongues poking through her hair. When Medusa angered, she evoked a stillness more unsettling than Roxanne's frantic pouncing or Dr. Hyde's pacing. Sometimes, when Medusa got this way, Roxanne felt like she might turn the world to stone.

"Don't my lady me," Medusa growled. "I'm not one of your women. And I am not your nursemaid."

Roxanne unfolded her fingers from her friend's shoulder. She tried to move slowly, so as to keep from startling Medusa. While Medusa's gaze did not work—not in the traditional sense—on Roxanne's and Dr. Hyde's altered humanity, it was unpleasant to look at. It made Roxanne feel the way she rarely felt: not only guilty but sorry for what she had done.

"What do you mean?" Roxanne said. "I don't think you're my nursemaid."

Behind Medusa, Dr. Hyde observed the situation with remarkable calm.

"You made this deal without consulting us. Fine. I was willing to accept that," Medusa said. One of her snakes burst free then buried itself once more in her scalp. "But you agreed to a caveat that you alone have been unable to keep. You like courting danger? I don't. I like having room to make mistakes. But you know what? The way you both behave?"

"What did I do?" Dr. Hyde said.

Medusa ignored them. "You both think I'm stiff. That I'm unlike you, unwilling to let loose. It's because of you. I'm not allowed to be careless. If I was careless, the three of us—all three of us!—would go down in flames."

Medusa breathed in and out. As though on cue, her hair unwove itself, the snakes hissing and unraveling to slither across her shoulders. They tested her skin with their teeth, then pulled back as though they understood themselves to be connected with her, as though they had only been testing self-destruction. Like Medusa, her snakes behaved.

"Now I've got a demon named Hector to kill. And thanks to you, thanks to you both, I have to be meticulous. I have to kill him like a surgeon."

"With a scalpel?" Dr. Hyde said. "I can give you a scalpel, if that's what you're worried about."

Medusa paused, a brief look of confusion passing over her face. "What? No. Meticulously. Without making a mistake. Weren't you listening to me?"

Dr. Hyde shrugged. "At first I thought you weren't talking to me."

Medusa stomped her foot. The whole laboratory shook, then stilled. One long crack split across the floor and up the side, and it began to open.

"I can't with you," Medusa said, and she fled the room with a flourish of her dress the way only an immortal creature from mythological times could flee: infused with the very essence of drama.

Chapter Thirteen

Mx. Hyde and Roxanne threaded their way through the mass of angry mosquitos that had gathered outside the laboratory. The moon above was no longer waxing crescent but waxing gibbous. They had missed first quarter.

"How long were we in there?" Roxanne said to herself.

"It felt like one evening," Dr. Hyde said. "But we're close to the Great Library of Evil, and if seasons move differently there—then who says moon phases cannot?"

Roxanne grumbled about the lost time as she and Dr. Hyde walked along the suspected path of the pipe they had used to enter the lab, but they could not be sure they were going the right way, as the ground gave no hint of where the pipe truly lay beneath the dirt.

Roxanne swatted at the terrible buzzing. "Do you think these are like, her children?"

Mx. Hyde scrunched up their face. Roxanne was always amazed at how fluidly the two halves moved as one even as they expressed themselves with their own small quirks: the raising of one brow, or a smile that could more easily be called a smirk.

"I'm quite sure she did not birth them," Mx. Hyde said. "She was still quite human, and I imagine her reproductive organs were still the same as a human's."

"Thanks for the biology lesson," Roxanne said.

For a while, they walked in silence.

"But we'll never know, will we? I'd have liked to get my hands on her for a proper study," Dr. Hyde said.

Roxanne could not help it. Though she was upset to have upset Medusa, though she was frightened for her friend's life if she had indeed gone off to fight the demon named Hector alone, Roxanne cackled. Mx. Hyde chuckled too.

"Oh, we've made a mess, haven't we?" Roxanne said as she threaded her arm in Mx. Hyde's. She stepped over a patch of toenail mushrooms.

Mx. Hyde looked back at the fungus as they walked away from it, but once they had finished their brief observation, they shook their head. "You made the mess, Roxanne. It was you, wasn't it, who drained those two innocents? You who failed to kill Needleskin?"

Roxanne stopped. It was an automatic reaction to Needleskin's name—her stomach lurched—and then she realized what her friend had said.

"I killed Needleskin," Roxanne said.

Mx. Hyde rolled their eyes. "You most certainly did not. But you will, won't you? Because if you don't, you won't have either of us around any longer. Listen, you know as well as I do that those lusty feelings disappear. What we have? It lasts multiple lifetimes."

"I know," Roxanne said, though she didn't—or she did. She wanted two things. She could have only one. Roxanne hated choices, and more than that, she hated being denied. "I know," she said, more firmly.

Mx. Hyde squinted at the sky, where a slip of horizon peeked over. "We should find someplace to rest."

"The morning always comes too soon," Roxanne said.

"Like a bad lay," Mx. Hyde said, then bit their lip. "It's been too long."

"You should try betrayal sometime," Roxanne said as her sharp gaze honed in on a little wood cottage, the kind that commonly held witches, in the near distance. "It keeps you young, you know."

Mx. Hyde pushed their friend forward. "Better run, or you'll burn up. I'll meet you."

Roxanne nodded. It had been a long while, as Roxanne tried not to leave her friends behind while they journeyed together, but Roxanne wasn't rusty. She held out her arms and willed them black and small and teased the air as she jumped into it. Who would choose a mosquito for trans-formation, Roxanne wondered as she flew to the cottage in the woods and prepared herself to woo the witch with-in. Everyone knew that bats were the sexier flyers.

The cottage's lamps were not burning. Roxanne touched down on the soft grass outside the cottage, presumably kept short by the goat who no doubt lived in a pen out back, and transformed back into a woman. Roxanne prod-ded her teeth, and when she inspected her fingers, the skin was clean of blood. It was risky to become a bat, or a cat, or a wolf—the form inhabited her so completely that she often woke with no recollection of her hunting—but it was riskier still to be out and about when the sun rose.

Roxanne snuck to the door of the cottage and listened to the nothing on the other side. But witches were sneaky too, and Roxanne did not trust that they didn't sense her coming and set a trap.

She threw open the door and rushed in encased with-in her vampiric blur, smelling for blood, but she smelled only stale bodily fluids. She stopped in the middle of the cottage's single room. All around her hung meat in the process of curing, and in the far back of the room, a few rabbits waiting to be skinned. The room reeked of white sage and juniper. The place was stuffy and small and crowded with the junk that witches kept around: jars of strange materials and materials made strange by the way the witches used them. Roxanne heaved a sigh of relief. The witch was clearly out.

Roxanne fell back onto the bed, the day drowse de-scending on her. She wanted to wait for Dr. Hyde so the two of them could secure the place, but she doubted she would be able to keep open her eyes. As she started to fall asleep, she saw in the hanging meat a pattern she had not before recognized: the parts did not appear to be animal, and they were moving. Roxanne reached to the window to pull shut the curtains there, and with the last light that peeked through, she saw a glint. The meat parts had been pierced with needles. She felt a familiar spike of fear in her as she drifted into her half-coma.

Chapter Fourteen

Roxanne dreamed. Upon the precipice of sleep, she had felt a fear, rare for her, but not wholly unexpected. Her sleep hours were the hours when she was most vulnerable to a stake through the heart.

In her dream, she stood in the middle of the field in which Medusa and she had lounged. She looked out at the horizon. It was on fire. She bent to tell Medusa, but her friend was nowhere to be found.

The chirp songs of the birds in the forest turned strange and otherworldly until they were clearly notes from a theremin. She felt his presence behind her.

"Do you want to know where she is?" The Guardian laughed. He grabbed hold of Roxanne by both shoulders. She could not resist. She was paralyzed. He hoisted her stiff body up onto his shoulders. He carried her across the landscape. She tried to scream, but she had lost her voice. "You will observe this dream, and nothing more. But do not worry. I will not hurt you."

Roxanne did not feel comforted.

As in a dream, time moved of its own volition, until they arrived at a great manor on a hilltop. Its façade was a warm tan stone with square towers that framed a long stretch of architecture covered by one straight line of blue roof. The front door was tall and round and green. Brittle ivy covered the stone like long dead hands, and a single light from the inside lit a window on the top floor. The house was surrounded by a wrought iron fence and hedges that had once been shaped and now, in their neglect, resembled battered wolves.

The Guardian carried Roxanne through the fence, past the gardens with their dead rosebushes, past the pond thick with scum and dead fish. He carried her to the door, and together they passed through it. The wood splintered into Roxanne's body, everywhere but her heart.

"I said I wouldn't hurt you," the Guardian said, "but I said nothing of the door!"

Her body ached as he carried her up a long set of stairs, down a hallway that smelled of dust and vomit, and into the lightened place: a library, where Medusa sat across from a perfectly ordinary man. Medusa had a book open in her lap. She read aloud from the story she had pulled from the Great Library.

"Well, that's not how it feels at all!" the man said.

Medusa shut the book. "Then how does it feel?" She did not seem to notice the Guardian and Roxanne, and Roxanne wondered if the scene before her were real. Certainly, it seemed as though Medusa was far from killing her victim.

"Sometimes, it's like a vacation? It's like the demon takes over, so I don't have to make the decisions or meet the social obligations I'm so often asked to fulfill," the man said.

"Sometimes?" Medusa said.

"Sure, other times, it is frightening. Like the worst type of losing control. When you're in a carriage that goes too fast around a corner, and you feel it tipping—and you know you might be on the verge of death. When you're paralyzed in your sleep and you fear you might never gain use of your body again. When you're with a young woman, perhaps the most beautiful woman in the whole history of the world, and you feel that nothing you could do would convince her to stay with you."

Medusa blushed, and her gaze found the rug beneath them. "I will stay with you, Hector."

Roxanne wanted to groan and laugh at the same time. Medusa had not changed since the dawn of time. Roxanne tried to wake up, but it seemed that the Guardian was intent on keeping her there for as long as he wanted.

She stood by the side of the room and watched them court like prudes. They smiled and giggled and inspected the rug as though trying to memorize the patterns there. And then Roxanne realized: every now and then, for the briefest of moments, they would look into one another's eyes.

Roxanne did not understand. The man did not turn to stone like he should. Damn whatever magic kept him from perishing! Medusa needed to kill him to stay here. Love wouldn't keep her here. Hector must go. But Roxanne could not move to suck the life from his neck. She appeared to be stuck here, frozen, until the night broke out and she rose. When that happened, she would run so fast she would blend into the wind. She would run so fast she'd have Hector's skin in her mouth before Medusa had time to protest.

"Shall we sleep now?" Medusa said. She touched Hector's arm. "It will be okay, I promise. I will be there for you."

He gulped, then nodded. "I'm ready," he said. "I know you'll take care of me."

Roxanne was moved then, as in a dream, to the foot of the bed where she stood without the Guardian to keep her there. Still she was unable to move, and being paralyzed without being in the presence of the paralyzing force was worse, somehow—it made her fear that she would never recover, not even if she defeated that terrible antagonist of sleep. She concentrated on each finger, each limb, trying to make herself move even a little bit, but she was frozen to the spot.

Medusa led Hector to his bed and set him down upon the edge.

"Sleep now," she said to him. "Remember, I am here."

He smiled weakly and lay back upon the sheets. He pulled his comforter over his body and settled in, seemingly peaceful for but a moment before a pall came over him and his muscles jerked him about. It was slow as first, then faster, as though he were being shocked by one of the evil doctors in the asylums. Then his body sat up, and it was clear to Roxanne that it was no longer Hector within it. The eyes were bright blue, and the hair was tangled and oily, as though his sweat had poured from his scalp as the demon took hold. Wounds opened in his skin and flexed in the casual lamplight. Medusa stood beside the bed and watched Hector transform.

"You must be the demon," she said.

The demon turned to face her. "You must be the whore."

"Is that any way to speak to a lady who is trying to help you?"

"The best way to help is to leave us," he said. "You can't fix us."

"I might be able to," she said. "If you can tell me what you want."

"I want fear." The demon opened his mouth, and black ooze poured out from between his lips and soaked the bed.

Medusa raised an eyebrow. "You're turning me on a little bit."

He frowned. "You're not afraid?"

"I've seen so much worse." She sat on the edge of the bed, where only minutes before her new beau had sat. "My best friends are monsters, you know. A vampire and a wicked doctor."

"Are you a monster?" the demon said.

"At times." Medusa's snakes came free. "I've been known to do terrible things."

The demon grinned with Hector's mouth. Its breath smelled like burnt bread. "Tell me about it?"

And Medusa turned to him and met him eye-to-eye. Her demeanor softened. The black ooze had soaked into the mattress and crept toward her, and it touched the edge of her derriere.

"Usually, these eyes turn people to stone." She reached out and cupped his cheek. Her hand sunk slightly into the rotting flesh. "I haven't always hated the power. I haven't always hated never letting others in."

"You lied to Hector," the demon said. It laughed. "You're no nurse come to care for us."

"Are you glad I lied?" she asked.

"I'm glad that I don't have to kill you," he said. "I'm glad that we can work together."

As Medusa's lips met the putrid lips of the demon, Roxanne faded back into her body—her true body, the one capable of so much more than standing still and watching and wishing she could grab the situation by its reins and ride it until it died from exhaustion. She forced open her eyes to find Dr. Hyde shaking her awake.

"How long have you been trying to wake me?" she asked.

"At least an hour," Dr. Hyde said. "Didn't you see?! You're not safe here! These parts hanging around—they're from vampires!"

Roxanne readjusted to reality and studied the room. Yes, she had seen that, before she fell into her deepest sleep. The parts had moved, and now a hand that hung from a hook on the ceiling opened and closed one finger as if beckoning her, and a foot struggled to stretch its toes, and a whole leg swung wildly in the back of the room, as if trying to escape.

"It was Needleskin," Roxanne said.

Dr. Hyde frowned. "Are you certain?"

"She's left me this message." Roxanne emerged from the bed. "She wants me to join her."

"It looks to me like she wants to cut you into pieces," Dr. Hyde said.

"Maybe. If I don't join her."

"Well." Dr. Hyde placed their hands on their hips and worried at their lip with their teeth. "Are you going to? Look, just tell us. If we have to go back to that place, to the underworld, then just let us know, so we can prepare or find some other way to stay here. Just be honest with us, Roxanne. Be honest in your intentions—be honest about your ability to resist."

"I'll try," Roxanne said. "I'll try to kill her. But right now, I'm not the one you need to worry about. I've just seen Medusa. And guess what? Her eyes were like fucking full moons."

Roxanne and Dr. Hyde could not leave until sunset, and so they took turns sleeping and keeping watch for Needleskin to return. She did not return, and neither did the witch who had once dwelled in the cottage in the woods.

Upon nightfall, they journeyed through the woods by foot until they came to a road. Down the road, past Roxanne's vision, she heard the galloping of two horses and the squeaking of a carriage wheel.

"It's our lucky day," she said to Mx. Hyde.

Dr. Hyde leaned over and pulled a couple of burrs off their pants. "We're two lucky monsters."

Once the carriage was within eyesight, Roxanne sprang onto the carriage driver. She ripped the woman's head to reveal the soft skin of the neck, then remembered. She looked out at Mx. Hyde waiting patiently at the side of the road, a look of resignation upon their face. Roxanne lifted the carriage driver and tossed her into the soft grass. She bid the horses to slow. From inside the carriage, she heard a sleepy voice: "Have we arrived?" The woman sounded beautiful.

"Will you take care of her?" Roxanne mouthed to Mx. Hyde. "I can't bear to look!"

Mx. Hyde smiled with half their mouth. "Roxanne, you are predictable."

"We all are," Roxanne said as Mx. Hyde moved to the door of the carriage and wrenched it open.

"I'm afraid this is your stop," they said.

The woman screamed, and Roxanne shivered. Mx. Hyde pulled the woman from the carriage and left her splayed upon the roadside as they climbed inside.

"Let's away!" Mx. Hyde called to their vampire driver.

"Yes, kind passenger," Roxanne said as she bid the horses forward. "To the manor!"

As she drove, she thought about Needleskin. The night air caressed her, and her skin felt sensitive to the touch. It was rare that she should experience goosebumps on her flesh or shiver from sensation, and both the wind and Needleskin had done that for her. She imagined running her hand along the sharp metal of Needleskin's needles. She remembered parting them and feeling the skin move and stretch as she snaked her long tongue between Needleskin's legs.

Roxanne called out to her companion. "Hyde, do you think monsters can love?"

Mx. Hyde said nothing. Roxanne thought her friend might be sleeping. She sighed and continued driving the horses until she glimpsed in the distance the old manor, its shadow stretching across the landscape as the moon lit it from behind.

Roxanne stopped the carriage a few paces from the door. She climbed down from the driver's seat and opened the carriage door. She pulled down the steps, though her friend did not need them. She held out her hand. Mx. Hyde placed their palm in hers and climbed down. They bowed as they planted both feet upon the gravel drive. Then they rose. They did not let go of Roxanne's hand.

"I know we can love," Mx. Hyde said. "Because I love Medusa. I love you."

Roxanne tried not to ache, but sometimes that was what kindness did to her. She did not respond. Instead, she looped her arm through Mx. Hyde's, and together they made their steady way to the entrance. Once on the doorstep, they shared a glance before Mx. Hyde grasped the lion's head knocker and brought it down upon the deep-grained red wood of the manor's front door.

Chapter Fifteen

The knock's massive sound reverberated. It was not met by the whisper of footsteps or the boom of a voice asking who was there. Roxanne was impatient. The time was ticking too quickly onward, and she was tired of the Guardian invading her dreams. She longed to sleep a whole day through, undisturbed by worry. She longed for things to go back to the way they used to be. Needleskin was still a persistent distraction, yes, but here, at the door to the manor inside of which her suggestible friend allowed herself to be wooed by suggestion, Roxanne understood the importance of their goal—and of their friendship. She kicked at the door with a force so strong her foot broke through the wood.

"You didn't even try the door," Dr. Hyde said as they helped Roxanne yank open a hole large enough for them both to climb through. "It could be unlocked, you know."

"I don't see you trying it." Roxanne tossed a sliver of wood into the dying grass.

Mx. Hyde grinned. "This way is more fun, of course."

Once they stood inside, they gazed up at the long staircase laid with a red carpet. The floors were made of white marble. When they stepped forward, and the open door to their left entered their eyesight, they saw that the man Hector was perhaps not as boring as they had thought. In the room that appeared to have once been a parlor, all manner of crosses hung from the ceiling and the wall.

"Best not to pry." Roxanne shivered.

"Amateur vampire hunter, you think?" Dr. Hyde said.

"Without a doubt." Roxanne grasped Mx. Hyde's hand. "Let's get up there."

"I'll go first."

Dr. Hyde led the way up the stairs and down the hall, searching along the way for any traps the man might have set for monsters like them. They had experienced their share of run-ins with hunters. The adventure that had killed Dr. Hyde and Medusa had been just such an occasion. Roxanne had survived only by fleeing the scene and hiding in the rafters. After the vampire hunter had left, she flew down and gathered her friends' relics and vowed to bring them back. Now Dr. Hyde took the lead.

They reached the door at which Roxanne had stood in her dream. It was closed, and from the other side, she heard grunting, a gasp, and a shrill scream. She shoved open the door and sprung inside, ready to save Medusa from the demon, but instead she stopped short.

Medusa had torn her chaste dress to let bare her ass, and she kneeled on her knees upon a red rug on the floor. Around her hips she had strapped leather, and she thrust with a new gasp into Hector, who lay on all fours to accommodate Medusa's movements.

"Whoa," Dr. Hyde said aloud, and at that, Medusa removed herself from Hector and turned. The phallus attached to her makeshift harness was one of her snakes turned to stone.

Medusa stumbled sideways. The snake broke free of the leather and tumbled across the floor while Medusa grabbed at her dress and pulled it down as far as it would go, which was just halfway down her thighs.

"You came," she said.

Roxanne raised her eyebrows. "Did Hector?"

Hector's head turned around on his neck. His skin had a greenish tint.

"Not yet." He cackled with his demonic voice.

"Don't let us stop you." Mx. Hyde swept to the bed and sat. "Please continue."

"I didn't know you had it in you," Roxanne said.

"Well, she didn't have it in her," Mx. Hyde said. "It was the other way around."

Medusa sighed. "Let's all have a laugh at my expense."

"It's good to see that you haven't gotten distracted." Roxanne crossed her arms. "Would hate for our whole plan to derail."

"Will you excuse me a moment?" Medusa asked Hector, who was still splayed with his ass in the air.

"Not at all, love," he said.

Medusa took Dr. Hyde by the arm and dragged them from the room. Roxanne backed out behind them, keeping her eye on the demon. Once they were in the hallway, Roxanne closed the door and turned to Medusa.

"Are you out of your head?" she yelled. "You're fucking a demon! The demon, in fact, that we are supposed to kill!"

Dr. Hyde shushed her, but Roxanne would not be shushed.

"You judged me, when you had no right to judge me!"

Dr. Hyde clamped her hand over Roxanne's mouth. Roxanne bit down, drawing blood, and Dr. Hyde pulled their hand back with a yelp.

"What do you have to say for yourself? I just . . . This is so unlike you!"

Medusa smiled like an idiot. "He can look in my eyes."

Roxanne screamed, then, and the whole manor shook.

"But wait! Stop!" Medusa stomped her foot, and the manor shook once more. Roxanne hushed so as not to bring the walls down. "It's okay that I love him. Listen: the Guardian is trying to trick us. Believe me when I say this. We cannot kill Hector. Please, listen. Please, let's talk this out like friends."

Roxanne was skeptical but curious. "Fine," she said. She recalled the room of crosses. "But you're sure your beau isn't going to try to kill me?"

"We know he's a vampire hunter," Dr. Hyde said.

"Was a monster hunter," Medusa said. "He's reformed, now that he's part monster. And that is exactly what I need to tell you: he is part monster. Only part. Which means, my friends—"

"He's part human," Dr. Hyde said. "Of course he is. He's only possessed. And if we kill the demon…"

"We kill the innocent." Roxanne felt her skin begin to heat. "We fail the whole terrible task."

Chapter Sixteen

The anger of the Monsters Three vibrated in the air. Outside, thunder rumbled. A great storm approached.

Roxanne was finished with bargains. She was finished with operating according to someone else's plan. She was finished with not drinking—with starving—with taking in only stale blood—with biting men. Over the last week, over the last month, she had tasted more men than she cared to taste in a lifetime. She was tired of being asked to choose between sex and love, between a lover and two friends. "I'm feeling rather tired." She faked a yawn.

Medusa nodded once, an uncommon surety in her expression. "I've thought of nothing else since Hector told me than taking that man down."

Dr. Hyde stroked their chin. "We'll need a plan, of course."

Roxanne nudged open the bedroom and peered in, past Hector, who lounged now in a chair by a fire, next to the window. Lightning lit up the night. It would remain night for a while yet.

"And a sleeping potion, actually. I'm not truly tired. I only said it to be dramatic."

Medusa squeezed Roxanne's shoulder. "We know, Rox."

The Monsters Three set up shop in the second-floor library. Hector provided the three of them white robes, and they wrapped themselves up and settled into the library's cushioned chairs.

"Roxanne's right," Dr. Hyde said. "We'll need a sleeping draught to keep us under, so we can face the Guardian for as long as we need."

"I have sedatives," Hector said.

Roxanne side-eyed the man. "M, your boyfriend's a vampire hunter."

Hector sighed. He looked human again, absent the green tint of rotted skin. "That isn't me anymore. I used to be be—it's how I made my fortune, selling my services! But honestly, I mostly performed what I named a 'de-vamping ritual,' where I held a cross to the chests of people who were ill and suspected of being turned. I chanted fake words. I sold potions made of common chemical to people who believed their loved ones required exorcisms. I really only killed one, two? Vampires, I mean."

Roxanne pulled her robe tighter, as though that would protect her. As though she needed protecting.

"Is that how you came to be possessed?" Dr. Hyde asked.

"I came across a real possession," Hector said. "Now I realize it's rude to kick people out of the bodies they acquired fair and square." He shrugged. "The demon's grown on me." As he laughed, his tongue lolled out of his mouth.

Roxanne pursed her lips. "I'll choose to believe you," she said. "But only because I have little choice."

Hector went to a small cabinet built into the library wall and pulled out several bottles of clear syrup.

"My family called in doctors at first. They gave me these, to keep me sedated. Before I killed them, of course."

"And your family?" Dr. Hyde asked.

Hector grinned sheepishly. "The same fate, I'm afraid."

Roxanne gave in to the unassuming charm of the half-man, half-monster her dear friend had grown to love in one day. He was better, at any rate, than Medusa's last brief love: the son of infamous monster hunter Professor Lee Vansing. That love affair had ended in a trap, and

Medusa shouldn't fault Roxanne her skepticism when it came to her romantic life.

Hector passed the bottles out. "One bottle each should do the trick."

"What's the chemical?" Dr. Hyde said, and Hector rattled off some words that bypassed Roxanne's brain altogether. The two discussed the details of ingestion and time to take effect and all the other boring bits that doctors and nerds liked to go on about. Roxanne rolled her bottle between her palms and allowed herself to feel relief that she would not have to kill Needleskin—and that she would not have to tell Medusa that she had not killed Needleskin already.

Once Hector and Dr. Hyde finished speaking, they instructed Medusa and Roxanne in the taking of the medication. They would swallow the whole bottle in one go, taking care to position themselves in a safe pose beforehand, for the draught would paralyze them limb by limb. The Monsters Three discussed their strategy of attack: they would go after the only weakness at which they could guess: his eyes. Roxanne and Dr. Hyde would steal his coins, and Medusa would gaze into his eyes.

It could work. He might turn to stone. Or they might strand him in the space between worlds, unable to pay for the journey back and forth. It was not a perfect plan— wouldn't they be forever haunted by him in sleep, even if he was, as they suspected he would be, unable to affect but dreams? They had no choice. It was the only plan they had among the three of them.

Medusa asked her beau to turn down the gas lamps. When the room was quiet, he lit a single candle, enough light for Dr. Hyde to see their own draught. Dr. Hyde, Medusa, and Roxanne lay in a circle on the floor, each of their bodies sticking out in one direction, a monstrous flower made of flesh. In her white robe, Roxanne felt like a little girl sleeping over with friends—with her only friend, that old friend, that dead friend. The friend who was the only thing she missed about being human. If only she had the chance to turn her. Roxanne swallowed the dryness in her mouth, and then, at the same time as her forever friends, the friends she was lucky to be able to share a monstrous eternity with, she swallowed the draught.

It tasted like divinity and peanuts. Terrible, but the aftertaste, the true poison underneath, was delicious on her tongue. She knew as it fled down her throat that such a treat was meant to kill a human, if slowly, if secretly. Hector had been right to murder his doctor before his inane medicine did more harm than good.

More harm than good, Roxanne thought, and she laughed at the words, which were like so much wishful thinking. Her neck relaxed, and her head settled into the wood underneath it. She fell through the wood, her body a ghost, and she tried to catch herself, but her death had gone differently than before. She was no creature of the night, except—she crashed against the floor of a room, crosses dangling above her head. She'd passed right through them, and now her ghostly body bore the smoking marks of the crucifix. What was she? Ghost and vampire both, it seemed. She tried to stand, and a man's hand caught her. He unleashed his claws of bone, and as her flesh hardened back to its true texture, its true weight, it formed around those claws. Roxanne cried out and clutched at what should have been the wound, but he was part of her, the same as her fangs were part of her, the same as her bloodlust. She leaned over and bit the Guardian on his throat.

His skin tasted like a dead frog's. He cackled as he ripped his claws from her body, opening up a wound far more gaping than any he could have made by piercing.

She screamed, and from behind him, an angry snake wrapped around his neck and yanked him away from her.

Roxanne gathered her strength. She could not give in to pain. She stood up and lunged through the dangling crosses toward him. They burned, but she burned stronger. She could see nothing but shadows moving before her. She grabbed hold of the only solid thing she could take hold of—his oar—and pulled it from his hand. She slammed it against his head.

"Watch out!" Medusa called, and her snakes slithered back into her hair. Roxanne could see again, now that enough of the smoke from her burning skin had cleared. She could see the whole expanse of room that led out to an old temple with crumbling columns.

The Guardian turned and struck out with his claw, attempting to cut a strand of hair from Medusa's head. Medusa turned to face the ancient temple and froze as still as stone. The Guardian seized his chance. He ran his claws deep down her back. She shrieked and fell to her knees on a ground that was now dirt.

"It's not real," Dr. Hyde said as they sprung onto the Guardian's shoulders. They stabbed wildly with their knife, but it tore into the Guardian's robes and did not pierce the flesh underneath. "M, ignore that out there! It isn't real!"

Roxanne had never heard Medusa talk much of her time before them, of her time before this world and all its glories. She knew only what the legends told her: that Medusa had once walked with gods.

"They could all look in my eyes," Medusa said now. "I was never alone. Until they decided I was a monster. Until they cast me out and destroyed my shrines."

"You're not alone now." Roxanne ran toward the mess of bodies, shoving the oar into the ground once she caught speed. She vaulted to where her friends fought, and with one swipe of his oar to his knees, she brought the Guardian crashing to the ground beside Medusa. Roxanne dropped the oar. Dr. Hyde held the man down. Roxanne ripped the copper coins from his eyes. "Now, Medusa!" Roxanne yelled, and Medusa turned her head slow as a creaking hour, all the way around her body, and stared the Guardian right in his fiery black eyes. Her snakes unfurled into their hissing mane.

"I'm not alone now," Medusa said.

But the Guardian did not turn to stone.

He reached up with his clawed hands and grasped Medusa around her neck. She choked. She clawed at his face. Dr. Hyde let the man go and tried to wrest Medusa from his grasp, but his grip was too strong. He held tight as what color remained fled from Medusa's face.

Then, in a moment, she was gone, ripped from the scene before them, and the Guardian's hands grasped at thin air.

He growled and sprang to his feet. "You'll pay for this," he said, slashing wildly with his claws. Roxanne dodged a swipe that came straight at her face. He slashed again. His claw caught in Dr. Hyde's suspender, and it tore. They screamed and ducked. He screamed in tune. Then stopped.

"Where are my coins?" he said. "I can't find my coins."

And Roxanne woke to Medusa pulling a needle from her arm. Beside them, Hector did the same to Mx. Hyde. Medusa's throat was bruised. Dr. Hyde's robes were shredded at the right shoulder.

"What—" Roxanne said, prodding her arm where the needle had pierced.

"Antidote," Hector said. "The demon helped me find it, back when my family used to treat me."

Though Medusa was clearly injured, she wore a smile so wide it threatened to eat her face.

"Did you think us dead or something?" Roxanne asked, uncomfortable with the proximity of so much unadulterated joy. Medusa held open her other hand, which had been pressed in a fist into the floor, steadying her body as she administered the antidote. From her now open palm tumbled two gold coins.

"And what?" Roxanne said. "He won't stop, not until he pulls you back." But Medusa's smile did not drop, and Roxanne furrowed her brow. "Wait!" She fingered the coins. "Yes! We have something of his! Medusa, you brilliant bastard. We can resurrect him!"

Medusa nodded feverishly, and Roxanne drew her friend down into the tightest hug they had ever shared and let the woman's musk, like smelling salts, bring her back.

Chapter Seventeen

It took them three nights to return to the edge of the forest that led to the Great Library of Evil. They slept in Hector's carefully concealed carriage, curtains drawn tight. He had joined them and given them the vehicle. After all, they had only five days until the new moon—and, as Roxanne was unlucky enough to overhear—he could not bear to lose Medusa so soon after they had found each other. They were soul mates, after all, even if it was in question whether they had souls at all. But Hector stood watch while they slept through the days and administered a syringe of stimulant when they tossed and turned, visited in sleep by the Guardian, from whom they all agreed to run at first glance.

When they arrived at the forest's edge, they left the carriage and traveled, as was required, by foot. Inside the forest, the world knew no common season, and so they walked across a patch of snow then moss then dead leaves then flowers that danced from full tree branches. Hector and Medusa stopped to kiss in the shower of pollen, and Mx. Hyde and Roxanne latched arms and mocked their love noises.

Finally, the Monsters Three and Hector reached the fence that surrounded the Great Library of Evil, which was lit by the light of a waning crescent moon. The gate was open. Black rosebushes lined the gravel trail to the door. As the Monsters Three and Medusa's possessed boyfriend walked along the pathway, Roxanne took in the scent of pond scum and brittle petals and a woman's sex. Her belly turned. She felt woozy, and was it from the lack of food or the lack of solid rest or perhaps some side effect of the poison she had ingested three nights prior?

"I smell it too," Dr. Hyde said. "Best if we're careful."

"I am always careful," Roxanne said, and she and her friend laughed until the lovebirds turned on them and accused them of laughing at their holding hands.

The front door was, as it always was for fiends, unlocked. They stepped across the threshold and into the unchanged foyer. The same spiderwebs graced the corners. The same dust coated the floors. The same smell of old books surrounded them.

"I love this place," Dr. Hyde said.

Roxanne scowled. "Really? I find it quite dull." And she did, for it was full of old books she had no desire to read. With the exception of the books they'd been given, the living monsters series, the books all detailed stale rituals and even staler villains—most of whom had a penis, or something resembling a penis, and did not interest Roxanne in the slightest, except when she was considering how to outdo them. It had been this impulse, to outdo the masters themselves, that brought the friends to the Great Library on that first fateful night. It had been desire to prove themselves worthy of a monster hunter like Professor Lee Vansing that made them tease him. They too had craved immortality. Like Dracula. Like the mummy and the swamp creature and the invisible one and the weird thing with all the hair on its shoulders and a bloody cut around its skull. They had read the memoirs of these monsters. In each, they were killed by the hunter—and in dying, they allowed themselves to someday return. In returning, they grew more frightening to everyone who had ever heard their names.

They had agreed, the Monsters Three, to that plan: to let themselves be killed by the professor but to leave some part of themselves behind, for accidental resurrection. But Roxanne had not wanted to die after all and, faced with the bodies of her two friends, she fled until it was safe to come down.

It was all her fault, this mess, and she was going to fix it. She was going to resurrect the Guardian, that bane of her existence, and his was to be the last masculine neck into which she would sink her teeth.

Roxanne sniffed out the librarian. It was easier this time, with her scent in Roxanne's memory. She was in some room full of books, but she was not dusting. Instead, she was building herself a web along one vacant wall.

"Looks cozy," Roxanne said as she slid into the room.

The Great Librarian of Evil pressed a button that made her glasses condense into an average human pair, and as she turned, her spider eyes retreated into her face, the skin growing back over them.

"It needs to be cozy," she said. "It's going to hold me for a long sleep."

"Hibernating, are we?" Roxanne said.

The Great Librarian sighed. "In a way, if you have to call it that. Hibernation is not a precise term, however. It's called the nocturnation, and it's largely a ritualistic gesture, undertaken to heal a creature of my kind from an ennui with the world around them."

"You have ennui?" Roxanne said.

"Roxanne, you've come here to ask me something." She stepped away from her wall. "I'm tired of my station here, and I'm even more tired of waiting for certain vampires to make their point."

Roxanne held the two coins out to the Great Librarian. "Can we have some of your blood again?"

"It's dangerous, what you plan to do."

"Pretty please," Roxanne said, her voice a monotone. When the Great Librarian still hesitated, Roxanne pocketed the coins and threw her hands up. "You knew we were coming. You knew we were going to ask. Why didn't you hide away, if you were going to refuse?"

The Great Librarian sighed again. "I'm not going to refuse. That bastard won't take me under, no matter how many times I die and now—" She gestured at the spiderweb, at the room around them. "Ennui! Immortality is boring, as I'm sure you know."

"I know no such thing," Roxanne said.

They set up, the Monsters Three and Hector and the Great Librarian of Evil, in the autobiography section, next to the stacks where those great monster men howled their life stories from the grave.

The Monsters Three waited for the new moon, which was still three days away, by chewing the white weeds that grew in a shaded area of the library's garden. The weed made them excitable and giddy, and for three days, they held hands and watched spiders move across the ceilings. The Great Librarian watched but did not partake in the weed. She did not sleep, she told them. When finally the day of the new moon arrived, the Monsters Three danced in celebration.

"You three really love the new moon," the librarian said.

Roxanne slowed her dance. The white weed's effects were fading, and she was irritated at the thought of explaining something as obvious as their reason for celebration.

"Now we can perform the resurrection," Roxanne said. "It had to wait until the new moon arrived."

The Great Librarian laughed. "Says who?"

"Says . . . everyone," Roxanne said.

"That's not true at all," the librarian said. "You can perform a resurrection anytime you want. Hell, they're performed on accident all the time!"

Roxanne blinked at the spider woman.

"If you'd read any books on the matter, you'd have read about how that myth has been busted for a long time now."

"You didn't think to tell us this?" Roxanne said. Her companions came to, slowing their own dances, but they were uninterested in the quarrel. "You saw us struggling to stay awake . . ."

"Oh, is that why you were eating white weed?" The librarian stood and walked to the table they'd set up. "I just thought you liked to waste away."

Roxanne had to keep herself from attacking the librarian, a task made more difficult by the strong scent of the librarian's blood as she sliced one of her arms with Dr. Hyde's knife and bled into a pewter chalice.

"Let's start then!" She gestured to the chalice. "This thing is supposed to be biblical or something." She let the blood fill it to the rim. "Came from the rare artifacts room."

"Will you show us that room, when it's all done?" Medusa asked, her voice wobbling. It was fear. Roxanne had heard it a hundred times.

"Better yet—I'll give you a skeleton key. You can have full reign of the place."

Dr. Hyde arched their eyebrow. "Truly?"

"You can all go wild," the Great Librarian said.

"We won't be here that long," Roxanne said. "After."

"Sure, sure." The Great Librarian pulled back her arm and handed the cup to Roxanne. She pressed her palm against her wound.

Roxanne raised the glass as though she meant to drink. She saw the spider woman flinch. But then she held the chalice above the two gold coins, side-by-side upon the table at which Roxanne had spent so many long hours, and poured. The coins were lost in the red deluge, until the blood slid down the grains of wood, to the edge of the table, to the floor, and the bloodied coins became once more visible.

The guardian's eyes grew underneath them. The coins rose up on the table as it happened. Then the rest of his skull, that terribly yellowed bone, then the skin, no longer rotten but fresh and full of color. The bone and muscle and veins grew from the air all down his long body. He was a thin man beneath the robes, unassuming. But as his robes returned to him, stitching themselves without hands or even needles or even thread, he was shrouded once more in mystery.

Roxanne thought she saw his hand twitch, and the oar grew from a seed clutched in his palm. He grinned with a set of full, sharp teeth as the oar completed its shape. Dr. Hyde grabbed their knife and hovered over him, waiting for his first breath so she could strike and take life from him just as it began. But he never breathed. Instead, he burst up from the table, knocking her back, and swooped across the room in a mess of fabric. He thrust his oar up toward the room's lonely window, and it returned to him in a shower of glass.

Roxanne and Medusa raced to catch him unarmed, but he moved too quickly, more quickly even than Roxanne. They turned to find him again. Roxanne caught sight of his shadow and stepped forward so she could see him. He had gathered ten daggers of glass from the broken window and was shoving them between his knuckles like blades.

She admired him his gory nature.

Roxanne rushed, a blue of red and pale, toward the shadows, and she was on him in a flash. He swiped at her with his finished hand, and blood flew from his fresh wounds onto her. The smell only made her wilder. Her fangs emerged. She bit at empty air, snarling. She was a creature. She was the night. She was everything he had said she was and more. She caught him by his neck and grabbed hold, and as he clawed at her with his shards of glass, opening wounds across her side, she did not let go.

Chapter Eighteen

"You are a wild one." Needleskin emerged from the shadows. She shoved her hands into the blur and caught hold of Roxanne's neck. She pulled her away from the Guardian right as Dr. Hyde, the Great Librarian, and Medusa formed a half-circle around him. Roxanne wailed as Needleskin threw her to the floor beside the stacks then kicked her body deeper into the darkness there. Roxanne's friends called out to her—but it was no use; the Guardian had engaged the three less-ravenous creatures in their own fight, squaring off against their formation.

Roxanne returned to herself as the smell of blood moved away. Needleskin did not smell like blood. No, the wounds she had made in herself had long since dried and were filled now with crusty remnants of dark gore. She still wore her needles all over her body and smelled, instead, like the stink in a woman's armpits. She knelt, and Roxanne watched the points of the needles on the backs of her legs press into her skin as her thigh met calf. She was a master of pain, and Roxanne felt herself pulled under by her presence.

"You've returned," Roxanne said.

"You haven't ditched your friends," Needleskin said.

"Good news! I don't have to kill you anymore," Roxanne said.

Needleskin cackled. "You never even tried."

She was right. Roxanne had failed at that. She struggled to regain her strength not because she felt she needed to save her friends—the Guardian had made clear that saving her friends was never something he was willing to let happen after all—but because she hated failing and all the weakness it signified. She pushed herself up and stared her lover-enemy in the eyes. Medusa would be proud.

"What is this, a game of goo eyes?" Needleskin said. "You can't have them and me at the same time, Roxanne." Needleskin gestured out into the room. Roxanne turned her head to look. The Guardian had beaten back the gang. Medusa and her boyfriend lay sprawled across the floor across the room, Medusa tending to some wound of his, while Dr. Hyde swung wildly with their skinny blade even as the guardian held them by their throat. The Great Librarian had disappeared entirely. "Come with me now. Make the world suffer. Or stay and help your friends." Needleskin held out her hand.

Roxanne stared down the outstretched palm. "Why can't I have both again? You'd like my friends."

"I doubt it," Needleskin said. "They don't understand pain the way that we do. They don't understand true evil. And I refuse to share you, with anyone."

Roxanne sighed. Some part of her had always known that she would turn out to be a soft-hearted harpy. If she thought about it, she could pull up the taste of Needleskin on her tongue, and it was a lovely must. The woman had given her the experience of a lifetime: a lust that did not fade after the blood dried. But there were two creatures who had given her other beautiful destructions, and they were in danger of dying another death. Even if Roxanne wanted to leave with Needleskin—and oh, how she ached between the legs to do so—she couldn't go at the expense of Medusa and Mx. Hyde.

"I mean, could you not wait for me, for like one measly hour?" Roxanne said.

Needleskin tried to narrow her eyes, but the pins holding them open made it look like a twitch of her eyelids. She reneged her offer of a palm.

"I won't forgive you, Roxanne," she said. "I won't forget you either."

Roxanne waved her old lover away. "Yes, fine," she said, coming to her feet. "Run off into the darkness."

"I . . . will . . ." Needleskin said, stepping back and back again until she disappeared entirely into shadow.

Roxanne's stomach boiled with rage. As far as she was concerned, it was not the fault of Needleskin that she could not follow her—and not the fault of the knocked-out Medusa or of Mx. Hyde—but the fault of the Guardian, that terror who had haunted their sleep for the last month. Roxanne pursed her lips so hard they numbed, and she turned on her heels to face the fight before her.

"I should tell you," Roxanne shouted at Medusa as she crouched behind the Guardian. "I didn't kill Needleskin."

"I knew," Medusa yelled.

"I'm glad." Roxanne sprung up onto the Guardian's shoulders, ripping her dress as her legs opened in the posture of a frog. A veil of red silk now covered his eyes, and Roxanne reached under her torn skirt and grabbed hold of his head with both her hands. She transformed, then, into a panther, and as her claws extended, they drove into his cheeks, cracking his cheekbones as they lodged into the skull.

The Guardian screamed. He let go of Dr. Hyde and his oar and reached both hands to try to push her off him. Dr. Hyde cried out as they landed on their ass.

Roxanne transformed back into herself; she wanted to be her truest self when she killed him. "How do you like it?" Roxanne said, and with her fingers pressing hard against both sides of his head, she snapped the Guardian's neck.

Chapter Nineteen

As the Guardian fell, Roxanne propelled herself away, landing on all fours on the ground in front of him. He shook the stone as he collapsed, and his hand crept out, searching for his oar, for the tool that would allow him to take himself across his river.

Dr. Hyde grabbed the oar and thrust it through the Guardian's chest. "Take it with you," they said. "We don't want your trash."

Roxanne scowled. "I mean, I would have liked it . . ."

"Oh, well, take it back," Dr. Hyde said, but as Roxanne looked back at the Guardian, his body faded into nothing.

Medusa glanced up from her boyfriend's prone body. Her face was wet with tears.

"Is he dead?" Roxanne's stomach dropped.

"No, he's fine," Medusa said. "It's just, he looks so peaceful when he's knocked out like this."

Roxanne and Mx. Hyde burst out laughing. They laughed until they were out of breath, and eventually, Medusa giggled as well.

"Why am I like this?" Medusa said.

"For a heart of stone, you sure are soft," Roxanne said. She hesitated, then continued. "I love you though. I love both of you. I know you don't think me capable of that—or you think me too reckless, or unpredictable, or—but I do love you both. I do try."

Now it was Medusa and Mx. Hyde who shared a look. Mx. Hyde wiped away their tears of laughter, and Medusa stood.

"We know." Medusa advanced toward them and grabbed them both by the hand. "We understand you, Roxanne."

Roxanne quickly spoke to keep her friends from going mushy. "But it's over now, this nonsense! We can go out again. We can wreak havoc! Let's start with the witches! I haven't eaten a witch in so long, and being in that witch's cabin gave me quite the craving. We could start there, if she isn't—" Roxanne stopped. Medusa and Hyde frowned. "Or you pick. You're the two who just got back from the dead, after all."

"It's not that," Medusa said, her voice nearly a whisper.

"Oh, for fuck's sake," Dr. Hyde said. "We don't want to travel, Roxanne."

"We want to rest for a while," Medusa said.

"Sure, of course." Roxanne worried at the thought, remembering her boring month waiting for the right time to bring them back to life. "We could find a town somewhere? Feed off the villagers one by one, until there's only the men left, then leave a whole city filled with men of stone! That could be wicked too!" She was getting excited about this plan, something new, something sinister that involved sneaking as well as slaying.

"I don't need to feed any longer," Medusa said. She gestured to her unconscious demon-man. "I found what I was looking for."

Roxanne waved her hand. "Just because you have one, doesn't mean you can't have more!"

"For me, it does." Medusa shrugged.

A single row of books cascaded off its shelf, revealing on the other side the Great Librarian of Evil trying to sneak out of the room. "Oops," she said, frozen in her spot, still ten paces from the door. The Monsters Three snapped their attention to her instead. "Keep on. I'm just disappearing quietly."

"You were hiding there the whole fight?" Roxanne said. "You're quite the coward."

The Great Librarian stepped out from behind the shelf. "I'm a librarian."

Roxanne wasn't sure what that meant, but she had bigger veins to drain. "So you don't want to feed anymore, M? You can still come with. Bring the man."

"I think we'd prefer not to," she said. "I think we'd like— for a while—a quiet life?"

"And when was this decided?" Roxanne raised her voice. "Fine. Dr. Hyde, looks like it's me and you."

"I won't be going either," Dr. Hyde said. "I don't need my serum anymore. Besides, death frightened me. I don't want to be forgotten. I want to write our memoirs, immortalize our adventures. In fact, I was going to ask the Great Librarian—is there space here for me to do that? I'd like access to research, if at all possible."

The Great Librarian's grin split her face as her spider eyes glistened. "There's plenty of space for you to write your memoir, Dr. Hyde. The collection would be the greater for it. There's rooms you can't even imagine. Some of them have beds and desks. Others have more specialized equipment. I'm sure you could even set up a lab!" She gestured at Medusa. "There are rooms fit for the possessed. Rooms fit for love. You would all be more than welcome to stay."

Roxanne felt like she was being staked through the heart. Or what she imagined that felt like anyway. It had never actually happened to her. She, of all her friends, was the only one who hadn't died. She had lived, damn it, and she had not lived—and fought for her friends to live—to waste away in a musty old library. But it was the right thing to do, to stay with them. It was the moral choice after all she'd put them through. She worked at the tear in her dress, tearing the rip until it spread across the skirt.

"Got a room with no windows? Maybe a coffin of some sort? Some sewing needles, thread? Maybe fabric. I can make myself a new dress."

"Roxanne . . ." Dr. Hyde said.

"It's fine. The dress is old. Needs an update. Why not show the legs as well as the neck? If it's good enough for old spiderwoman here."

"No, Roxanne." Dr. Hyde clamped their hand on Roxanne's shoulder. "I won't let you stay."

"I won't either," Medusa said.

"I'll jump on the bandwagon, sure," the Great Librarian of Evil said. "I've got no rooms for you, vampire."

"What?" Roxanne stopped what she was doing. Half of dress hung off by a thread of fabric. "I did some shitty stuff, but we all have, haven't we?"

Medusa wrapped her arms around Roxanne. "You're not being punished."

"No punishment," Dr. Hyde said. "It would be cruel to keep you here. Like caging a lion."

"They cage lions all the time," the Great Librarian said.

"Doesn't make it less cruel." Dr. Hyde added their arms on top of Medusa's. "You belong out there."

"We know you," Medusa said. "How many times do we have to say it? You deserve to maim and murder. You deserve to make a mess."

Roxanne's stomach turned. Maybe it was appreciation. But maybe it was hunger. How long had it been since she'd eaten? She glanced at the space on the floor where the Guardian's body had lain. She should have drained him. She sighed.

"I'll miss you both," she said. "You glorious fiends."

"You'll come back for us," Mx. Hyde said. "Someday you'll have to come read this book I'm going to write."

Roxanne would never read it, she felt sure of that. Not unless Hyde strapped her to a chair and pinned open her eyes. Roxanne grinned. That didn't sound half bad, minus the reading part. Maybe they could work together on it, come up with some way to make the reading part more appealing. For certain, Roxanne would return to see what became of Medusa's demon boyfriend once the demon left his shell of a body behind and Medusa accidentally turned him to stone. Maybe Medusa and the demon would decide together to make the world their playground, and the humans in it their playthings—maybe he would be the one to finally turn her wicked. Given space, Dr. Hyde was sure to come up with some nasty experiment. They'd thirst again for some bodily fluid or another. Roxanne wouldn't be without them her whole life. That was the truth. The hope. The honest hope.

"Are you crying?" Medusa pulled away. Blood had soaked through the shoulder of her dress.

Roxanne reached up to her eye and wiped away a red tear. "I'm just rotting from the inside out." She kissed Medusa then Mx. Hyde on their lips. "Don't you worry about me. I'll be just fine."

"We know," Medusa said, exasperated at the repetition.

"You always are," Dr. Hyde said.

Chapter Twenty

Roxanne slept one more night in the Great Library of Evil. Before she left, she toured the rooms that would become her friends' domains. She imagined them as they would become: copper tables lining the walls in Mx. Hyde's lab, which was attached to a bedroom. In the bedroom, one single window beside which Mx. Hyde would drag a great Wooton desk of mahogany with a leather inlay. The kind with hidden compartments in which Hyde could stow away the tools of that old trade, murder. A bed in the room's corner with two sides and a gas lamp on a table for reading well into the night. A little cupboard of their favorite snacks. A bureau with enough suspenders to last a lifetime.

Medusa's room had a bay window with doors that opened out to let in fresh air. Roxanne imagined the lover's nonsense that would float from that window, the acts of desperate fucking that would occur upon the four-poster bed surrounded by a lace curtain. The sheets and drapes and blankets were all white, and Roxanne smirked to think of the demonic messes that would mar the perfect linens—fluids from the demon's mouth and more.

Roxanne commended her friends their futures and said her goodbyes. She left in her freshly torn red dress. It was a new fashion, and she closed her eyes as the cool night air blew upon her bare legs. She wanted to walk a while and so she did not transform right away, delighting instead in the feeling of going without needing to be anywhere. She was headed to find dinner—and she could take as much time as her body would allow.

Roxanne felt a tickle on her neck, behind her hair. She reached up and swatted at herself. A tiny spider tumbled from the webbing she'd stretched across Roxanne's back. The Great Librarian of Evil transformed as she fell, her human legs only barely catching herself as she planted her feet on the cobblestone walk.

"What are you doing here?" Roxanne said, her sharp teeth on alert as she identified the best place to pierce the stowaway's skin.

"I'm coming with you," the woman said.

"But your library," Roxanne said.

"I've accomplished all I sought to accomplish there," the woman said. "I'd like to do more than catalog monstrosity now. I'd like to live it."

"But you heard that in there. I've outgrown friendship. Or friendship has outgrown me."

"Well, I suspect it's less friendship altogether and more those particular friends. You know, most friends do eventually go their separate ways. Time to forge your own path. Which is what I'm attempting. We have that much in common."

"But I don't need new friends," Roxanne said.

"Well, if it helps, I don't like you one bit," she said.

"Thank you," Roxanne said. "I hate you too."

"Oh good! Then that's settled."

"You want to travel with someone you hate?" Roxanne said.

"I think you'll find, Roxanne, that I hate everyone. It's nothing new for me to spend all my time with my enemies."

Roxanne sighed. The woman wasn't going anywhere, that was clear, and she had her perks, her hourglass body, her venom. Her complete knowledge of the world and all the dark things in it. Roxanne studied her lips. They were plump and pink, and Roxanne imagined that having a companion on the lonely road would not be the worst thing. Depending on what Needleskin wanted, what Roxanne wanted once she found Needleskin, the Great Librarian, Librarian No More could be an offering—or an asset against the heathen's revenge.

"You can come," Roxanne said. She would have to walk the whole way. "I need to feed."

"Absolutely," the librarian said. "I understand what a vampire is, what a vampire does. You know, we could be great help to one another. Me, I know everything there is to know about the darkness of the world. You, you know—" The librarian laughed. "Well, I'm sure you'll be helpful to me as well, eventually."

Roxanne did not laugh, but she was not annoyed either. This woman, this all-knowing creature, had lived only in twilight, and she was in for the rude awakening of the reality of the moonless hours. Roxanne would love watching her fail, maybe even die. Roxanne's stomach growled. And maybe it was hunger—it was hunger, had always been hunger.

In fact, why wait to watch the woman die? The librarian had returned before, and would she not return again? It sounded like a fun game, regardless of outcome or consequence. As the moon disappeared behind clouds and the music of the journey wilted, Roxanne studied the librarian out of the corner of her eye until a beat returned to the air. As the wind began to crescendo and the forest around them performed its night theater, Roxanne bared her fangs and lunged toward the shrieking sustenance.

Acknowledgments

I've been lucky to know a lot of glorious fiends who have been instrumental in supporting me through the writing of this novella and throughout my writing life.

Thanks first to my editor, Darin Bradley; my agent, Hannah Bowman; and my publisher, Underland Press. They provide the essential ingredients for the publishing potion.

Thanks to my family: my parents, Jenny and Eddie; my husband, William; my sister, Rachel; my nephews, Silas and Ian; my brothers-in-law, Tommy and Andrew; and my parents-in-law, Carolyn and Bob. Family is the blood that sustains the hungry undead.

Thanks to the writing community with whom I've had the honor of pillaging the wealth of stories that have come before: my coworkers; Cassandra Rose Clarke; Holly Walrath; D.L. Young; Bill Ledbetter; Michelle Muenzler; Layla Al-Bedawi; Julie C. Day; Michael DeLuca; Katie Crumpton; Mur Lafferty; Tony Pisculli; all my remaining Stonecoast friends and teachers including Jim Kelly, Elizabeth Hand, and Theodora Goss; Sam J. Miller; the AudioJack crew; Karen Bovenmyer; Scott Andrews; Sarah Pinsker; Kellan Szpara; Bo Bolander; all my Art & Words folks; Spider-friends; Kendra Fortmeyer; the Wordos; Jordan Kurella; and Aliza T. Greenblatt.

Thanks to Chris Panatier, whose gorgeous and grotesque artwork perfectly captured the book's heart.

And thanks to my coterie, for whom I would easily make a deal with the devil to resurrect: Emily, who read all my drafts; Cera, whose spooky music recommendations are an inspiration; Jamie, whose kindness has kept me going; Janna, whose dark sensibilities influenced my childhood; Becca, whose positive energy lifts me up; Jim, whose twisted humor matches mine; Chris and Kim, whose Halloween parties set the season; and Alicia, whose love of books is infectious.

About the Author

Bonnie Jo Stufflebeam's fiction has appeared in over 90 publications such as *Le Var Burton Reads* and *Popular Science*, as well as in six languages. By night, she has been a finalist for the Nebula Award. By day, she works as a Narrative Designer writing romance games.

She lives in Texas with her partner and a mysterious number of cats.

Printed in Great Britain
by Amazon